I0619376

VERONICA'S STORY

an Expired Reality novella

David N. Alderman

ISBN: 978-1-945712-40-1

Visit **DavidNAlderman.com**

CHAPTER 1

Lazy Clouds
Friday, February 6, 1998

U p in the fathomless blue sky, clusters of white puffy clouds drifted lazily by. They seemed to have no care in the world, floating wherever the wind blew them, wherever life carried them. They took shapes today, unique shapes that clouds didn't normally take.

One cloud took the form of a beautiful flower, the stem of which crossed the entire length of sky. Though most clouds were white, Veronica Amorou imagined this one was violet, her favorite color.

Most of her friends didn't think she had too much of an imagination. Certainly not with the clouds. She loved fashion design, but the only person who really seemed to care about any of that was Carrie Green. David Corbin had little interest in her fashion passion, and her twin brother, Sean, always made it clear he had no interest in the clothing line she was trying to piece together.

Veronica's long, dark hair spilled out like midnight-colored ocean waves eating at the winter grass underneath her head. She loved to visit this park on cool winter days like today, both to be alone with her thoughts and to enjoy nature before the spring—

and then summer—heat became somewhat unbearable later in the season. It was a fine day to wear blue jeans and a purple T-shirt, though Veronica would have enjoyed donning a nice summer dress if she didn't think her legs would freeze in the cold.

Another cloud drifted by, and Veronica took notice, almost immediately attributing a form to it: a black butterfly. She smiled at the thought. Something about the winged insect seemed familiar to her, but she couldn't pinpoint why.

She closed her eyes and inhaled the scent of rain, her heart rejoicing at what she perceived might be a coming storm. Here, somehow, she had little to no cares. She felt as if she resided within a place that was safe from the outside world. A sanctuary of sorts offering her protection from the cancerous afflictions that plagued the city of Lysallis and all of Enera.

She took a deep breath. She wanted to keep daydreaming, wanted to keep pondering what could be. High school was long behind her. Her and the rest of the Lazerblades had already saved most of Anaisha from whatever crazy criminal master-minds wanted to take it over, aside from Mr. Big. But even he didn't seem to be up to anything at the current moment.

When she opened her eyes, she saw a massive cloud skating through the blue atmosphere overhead. This one was in the shape of a massive castle. Veronica imagined herself as a damsel in distress, high up in the castle behind the great stone walls. She wore a long, purple dress, and her hair flowed to the floor, the strands garnered with brightly colored violets. Some daring young man entered her daydream, arriving at the castle to rescue her from an evil prince or a horrible dragon. She couldn't decide. There were so many evils in the world, it took her some effort to decide which one she wanted to be rescued from. The hero didn't care what evil harassed her. He would slay whatever ailed her and then he would sweep Veronica up in his arms and carry her off to some far-off land where they would live happily ever after.

She sat up in the grass, dismayed that her daydreams were just that: dreams. Fantasies. She glanced around the park. The few people who lingered were now leaving, no doubt distraught over the dark storm clouds that were beginning to fill the sky. She welcomed those clouds, welcomed the rain, welcomed the storm. She dismissed her fantasies with one final grin, imagining how much fun it would be to design the dress in her castle daydream.

She stood to her feet and stretched, breathing in the cool, rain-scented air. The dark clouds were all around her now, filling the sky with their awesome presence. She wondered what David and Carrie were up to. She knew her brother, Sean, was probably off on a date or getting himself into trouble. David and Carrie though were items of interest to her, if not for the simple fact that they had become Veronica's own personal soap opera with the way they each refused to tell each other how much they adored one another.

Veronica walked across the empty grass field and left the park, taking the sidewalk into the suburban neighborhood. The late afternoon sun was busy escaping the dark storm clouds, bright oranges and reds bleeding across the streets, casting shadows all over the place. She loved this time of day, entryway into night.

She cursed the situation with David and Carrie. She had become quite sick of hearing (constantly) about their on again, off again feelings for one another, and she wished they would just get it over with and be with each other already. It was sickening how they denied their feelings for each other. Especially David. He was the man, he should be the one to step up and take control of the situation, right? Veronica chuckled to herself. Women *were* empowered nowadays, and it wouldn't make a difference if David or Carrie made the first move—as long as one of them did and soon. But she would have liked to see David step up to the plate and confess his feelings. If one of them didn't say something to the other soon, Veronica would be forced to tell each of them their feelings for one another, if for no other reason than to preserve Veronica's own sanity.

Veronica remembered Carrie telling her she had a date this evening. Some weird guy she met at the grocery store. He asked her out over a bundle of carrots in the produce section. Veronica sighed. *Well,* she thought, *at least that guy seems to have more guts in that area than David.*

David. She had to figure out a way to keep a better eye on him.

Years ago, he saved her life fighting a villain in the massive clock tower in South Ryshard. Veronica pledged her own secret life debt to him and since then, had kept a close eye on him. But now a close eye wouldn't be enough. Mr. Big was still out and about, probably rebuilding his empire. Nobody had seen him in months, but that didn't mean he wasn't up to something. When the time came, Veronica knew she would more than likely have to break the truce her and the others had to not use violent means to save Anaisha. She would have to learn how to use weapons, if simply to protect David's life. She wasn't sure how she knew this or what her reasons for allowing her thoughts to travel down this road were, but that's where she was at, and she wasn't going to apologize to herself or make excuses for it. The world itself was changing. This was another thing she knew but wasn't sure *how* she knew. Something in the air she breathed, something in the feel of the wind and air.

Something nefarious was coming their way.

She shook those thoughts, passing through the neighborhood as she made her way back home. She watched mothers and fathers call their children in from playing in the driveways. The wind started to pick up a little, and with it, small freckles of rain misted Veronica's face and bare arms.

David. He entered her mind again as she stopped in her tracks. An SUV had started to pull out of their driveway without checking their mirrors. Veronica waved them out as the middle-aged woman mouthed the word 'sorry' from the driver's seat. Once her vehicle was on the street, Veronica continued along the sidewalk.

She realized that deep down inside of her, she had a true love for David. Not a romantic love—she didn't think—but a respectful love. One that went beyond the barriers of David's sometimes stubborn ways. A love that would allow her to sacrifice her own life for him someday. She didn't know why this feeling came so strongly, it just did.

There seemed to be a great many things she had an uncanny intuition about but could not explain. She called it—for lack of a better word—her instinct, but she knew it had to be more than that. It felt more like a foreboding of things to come. Grave things to come. Always dark.

Veronica reached her family's one-story house and walked up the driveway. The surface of the concrete was marred with oil stains from her father's junker vehicle that he used to commute to work every day.

She walked along the concrete path that led to the front door, observing the lilacs that graced the edges of the path. She had planted those a month ago and was happy with how fast they had grown. She would need to remember to water them tonight. Even though they weren't known to grow well in winter, the lilacs Veronica had planted were special hybrids that resisted frost and seemed to thrive in the cold weather.

She entered the house, finding it empty. *Perfect.*

She grabbed a tall glass of cold water from the kitchen faucet and drank it up, her mind trying to remember when anyone would be home.

The purple telephone on the kitchen wall rang, startling her back to reality. The glass of water slipped from her grip and crashed against the side of the marble island scattering glass every which way. She mumbled a curse or two and tiptoed around the shards, grabbing the phone from the wall.

"Hello?"

"Veronica?"

"David?" Even she noticed the bounciness in her own voice.

"Hey, didn't think you'd be home. I have a favor to ask of you."

"Yeah?" It felt nice to hear his voice. She had been alone with her thoughts all day and though it was comforting and relaxing to have a day to oneself, she could only tolerate it for so long. She loved to be around others, to mingle with strangers and hang out with her friends.

"I have a blind date tonight and was wondering if you wouldn't mind keeping it a secret from Carrie. She's been a little defensive lately whenever I mention other girls. I'm not sure why."

A blind date? Secret from Carrie? She was already holding Carrie's date a secret from David. This was ridiculous.

"You're not sure why?" she started. Then she reminded herself that it wasn't really her place to meddle. Not yet. She figured she would give them until the summer and then she would burst both of their bubbles. Then whatever was meant to happen could happen and they could move into the fall without having to wonder about one another. "I suppose," she said, correcting herself. "I'll keep it a secret. Where did you find this blind date?"

"Online. We're going to the Lysallis Bowling Alley. I thought it might be fun. We're going out before that to The Steak House."

Hm. "What time are you going out?"

"Uh, I'm picking her up at 7."

"Well, that's sounds like fun."

"Hope so!"

"Alright, I'll talk to you later," Veronica said, eager to end the call. Now it just felt awkward.

"Hey, Veronica?"

"Yes?"

"Thanks for keeping this a secret. It's not really that big a deal, I just don't want to…I don't want to upset Carrie. You know?"

"Sure."

"Thanks. Talk to you later."

She slammed the phone onto the receiver and then looked down to the glass shards spread across the kitchen floor. She knew she should clean them up but had no desire to. Who cared? Her parents were out of town, and she knew she was going to have to get ready to go out tonight, to keep an eye on David. A blind date sounded like trouble. Veronica remembered David's last date…Jennifer. Mr. Big's niece. That was a nightmare.

Veronica grabbed the broom and dustpan and swept up the glass. Then she went into her room and started shuffling through outfits in her closet. She would have to keep a low profile tonight, stay out of David's field of vision. If he ever found her following him around, there would be a lot of explaining to do, or at the very least a crafty excuse that Veronica didn't think she had the intelligence to put together. Even she knew that what she did—tailing him on his dates—was a bit strange, but how else could she keep a close eye on him?

She picked out a blue blouse and black jeans. She took off her T-shirt and stared at herself in the mirror for a moment. She eyed her breasts that sat nestled in a black bra, swearing to herself that one of them was lopsided. She shifted them, relieved that they remained even, and told herself it was just her imagination. She slipped on the blue blouse and buttoned it up. Then she slipped off her blue jeans and felt her legs for stubble. They were still pretty smooth. Satisfied, she slipped on the blue jeans and then slid her feet into her blue and white sneakers.

She smiled at the mirror, satisfied with her ensemble. It was missing something…

She grabbed a blue flower clip off the top of her dresser and, after collecting her hair into a bunch atop her head, snapped the hair accessory in. *There!*

She stared at the flower and sighed. *This isn't low profile*, she reminded herself. She pulled the hair clip out and let her black hair fall across her chest. She unbuttoned the top button of the blouse and let the top of her breasts breath a bit.

She suddenly realized, amidst getting ready to tail one of the only men in her life (besides her brother, Sean) on his blind date, that she wanted someone in her own life. She wanted a gentleman, someone who would accept her for who she really was. She knew she could be moody, direct, and sometimes incredibly introverted. At other times she could be very extroverted. It all depended on a variety of factors. Overall, though, she considered herself to be very consistent in her nature. She was loyal, reliable, and could be counted on.

And she *never* lied. She could keep secrets, but she would never lie. That's why it was so important that David never realized what Veronica was doing. She couldn't lie to him. *Especially* not him.

She grabbed her purse and glanced at the digital clock on her nightstand. It was already six-thirty. By the time she arrived close enough to David's house to follow him, it would be around seven.

***

The evening played out in a very predictable way, beginning with dinner at The Steak House in downtown Lysallis. It was a pricey restaurant that Veronica had only been to once before. The place had warm lighting, hardwood tables, comfortable booths, and top-tier service. The food was fair, though Veronica felt the quality didn't meet the exorbitant prices.

David and his date sat in a corner booth toward the back of the restaurant. The place was packed, but Veronica had managed to tip the host to get a booth not far from David's.

David's date wasn't anything to write home about. She was about five-foot-eight, had long blond hair, and was fairly thin. She wasn't as thin—rather fit—as Veronica, but she wasn't overweight. She had a pudge belly, and her legs looked like lines of coleslaw that someone plopped on a plate at a family dinner.

Veronica didn't think of herself as thin, necessarily, just in shape. She took walks every morning for about a mile and rode her bicycle every—rather *almost* every—night around the neighborhood. She tried to eat right.

Was all of that enough? Why wouldn't some random guy out here in Lysallis want to be with her? Or was it her desire not to be with the guys of Lysallis? The only person she really found capable of even satisfying her needs in a mate was David, but his mind, body, and soul…well, his mind and soul…were taken by Carrie. Until the end of time, no doubt.

The date (Veronica managed to catch her name—Brittany) carried herself as if she sat in a cubicle, processing reports on a computer all day, her back hunched, her gait somewhat sloppy and stumbly. She giggled and laughed like a drunk and threw her hands all over David as if she didn't know what to do with her body when she was around him. David seemed to repel her advances somewhat successfully, nudging her away or drawing himself a good distance from her. But boy was she smothering.

After dinner, they headed to the bowling alley in downtown Lysallis. Since it was a Friday night, there were lots of teenagers horsing around the alley and it made Veronica feel claustrophobic, although the crowds did help her to blend in. She watched David and Brittany from an inconspicuous seat in the noisy arcade as she sipped on a Dr. Soda. The couple was on lane seven, and at the moment, Brittany was conning David into 'teaching' her how to bowl. *How hard is it to roll a ball down a strip of flooring?* He had his arms wrapped around her thin waist. *Ech. That should be Carrie.*

Veronica knew it was an intentional move for the girl to wear a short skirt and form-fitting T-shirt this evening, even though it was the middle of winter. She seemed to be firing on all cylinders with the seduction, but Veronica also knew David had some level of integrity and wouldn't fall for the girl's wiles…at first, anyway. Would Veronica intervene if things got too heated? She felt if it was necessary, then she might cross some personal boundaries.

You're here to keep him safe from physical harm, she reminded herself, *not emotional.*

"What have we got here? Look at this, boys! Dang!"

Veronica turned to her right and spotted three college guys, all of them with mugs of beer in hand, standing in a cluster by the *Galaxy Shooter* game. She turned away from them and returned her attention to David and his temptatious companion.

"She just blow you off?"

Veronica felt the men enter her personal space and gather directly behind her. The smell of alcohol wafted into her nostrils, and she cringed. She hated the smell of beer.

A warm breath fell on her left ear. "Hey, baby. What's your name?"

Veronica took a sip of her soda and set the cup down on the *Chronic Fighter* arcade machine before turning toward the man. He was tall—at least six and a half feet, and he had a bowl cut hairstyle and a scar above his left eye. Most likely the brawler of the group.

She grinned. "Do you honestly think my parents would be stupid enough to name me Baby?"

The man's eyebrows arched, though the one above his left eye did so at a crooked angle because of the scar. "What?"

His companions drew back from their friend and started to feign playing on the *Galaxy Shooter* game.

The man with the scar took a quick, jolting sip of his beer and slammed the mug down on the *Chronic Fighter* game. "Are you getting smart with me?"

Veronica glanced over her shoulder at lane seven. David and Brittany were still bowling. She turned back to the man. "Scoot along, tough guy. I'm not interested."

His face flushed. "Not interested?" He drew closer to her. Her eyeline fell at the place the bottom button of his polo shirt fell open, exposing strands of dark chest hair. She imagined this man was probably a walking, talking monkey with no clothes on.

One of his buddies put a hand on his shoulder. "Jake, take it easy man. It's not worth it."

Jake ran his massive palm through his short hair and fumed.

His eyes wandered down to Veronica's blouse.

She crossed her arms over her chest, wishing she hadn't given her breasts room to breathe. "I suggest you get away from me."

"Are you—Are you—threatening me?"

She sighed and rolled her eyes, blatantly so he could see.

The man closed his eyes and grimaced, as if he was trying to hold back some urge to kill her. Veronica realized that with the man's strength, build and size, that she would pose almost no opposition to him, especially with David in the same vicinity and her wanting to stay incognito.

Jake's two friends were behind him now, each one holding one of the man's shoulders to restrain him from moving any closer to Veronica.

Jake shifted his body out of his friend's grip and stepped closer to Veronica—so close that she could feel the warmth radiating off the thick skin on his face. He reached out, quick as a viper, and clutched Veronica's neck, slamming her up against the *Chronic Fighter* arcade machine.

Her heart nearly leaped into her throat, but she fought to remain calm. They were in a public place, and the last thing she wanted to do was draw undue attention to herself. The other patrons of the bowling alley seemed consumed with their own affairs, though one or two people did look her way.

When he spoke, Veronica could see that some of his front teeth were chipped, no doubt from other senseless fights he had picked with other undeserving victims. His breath was rank. She could smell not only the beer, but a mix of onions and peppers as well.

His friends fought to pull him away from her, but even they didn't seem to be strong or entertaining enough to draw him away.

"Listen good, my pretty little thing. If I take time out of my evening to come over here and talk to you, you talk back like a proper lady, not some wench from Merena. Now, I'm looking for some fun tonight. You look like fun. So you and I are gonna—"

His friends managed to yank him away from Veronica, breaking his hold on her neck as he stumbled backwards and fell onto his back on the stained arcade carpet.

She fell to her knees, gasping for air, as she rubbed the pain from the surface of her neck.

She watched as Jake struggled to his feet and turned to his friends, pushing them back. "Get off me!!"

Veronica stood, anger boiling within her. This man was a menace and needed to be taught a lesson. She figured she wasn't the first or only woman he had ever attacked, and if he wasn't stopped, she wouldn't be the last.

Jake attempted to lunge at Veronica again, but one of his friends yanked his shoulder and pulled him back again. "Dude, you wanna get arrested?"

Jake spun around and punched his friend in the face, knocking him to the floor. The other friend tackled Jake and they started brawling. Veronica peered over her shoulder and saw that they had the attention of the entire bowling alley now—except David and Brittany, who were nowhere to be found. Veronica did spot a security guard booking it from the front of the establishment, his hands fumbling to keep his oversized pants up as he ran.

Veronica fled the scene, escaping through a dense section of the surrounding crowd. She exited the bowling alley through the parking garage just in time to watch David and Brittany getting into David's white four-door sedan. She heard the car sputter and stall as David attempted to start it. This gave her time to make her way out to the street where she had parked her own vehicle.

Veronica made it to her two-door car and started it gracefully just as David's car sped past her.

She followed him down a few streets and then into another parking structure, where David drove his date to the very top. Veronica had suspected David would come here. This was the tallest parking structure in Lysallis, and one could see the entire city skyline from the apex of the parking structure. He had even taken Veronica up here once…to talk about his feelings for Carrie.

He parked at the top, and Veronica parked two levels below him. Then she made her way into the stairwell, which she took to the top floor. It was a spot in which she could easily keep an eye David while also staying out of sight. She could make an excuse as to why she was at the bowling alley if David managed to spot her there, but what excuse could she use for being at the top of the same parking structure as him and his date? Veronica was certain if David found out she was tailing him to this particular spot, it would seriously damage their friendship and break whatever trust he had in her.

David and Brittany walked to the edge of the parking structure as David pointed out the tall blue Bank of Lysallis building that rose higher than the other buildings in the city. He always seemed to be so mesmerized by the neon lighting of that particular building, and Veronica felt drawn to it, as if it had something to do with their future.

Small lights hanging from the cement walls illuminated the stairwell just enough so Veronica could scan the stairs below to make sure nobody was coming up behind her. The last thing she needed was someone sneaking up on her when she wasn't paying attention, though this particular parking structure wasn't as busy because there weren't many Friday-night-friendly businesses around this part of the city.

Veronica sat on the top step and sighed as she watched David and Brittany gush over one another. Veronica felt…jealous?

No, that couldn't be it. She rarely felt jealous. She would like someone of her own to gush over. Heck, she'd settle for having a life in general. With Big MIA, Veronica really didn't know what to do with herself. She felt a sick depression sink in at the lack of social life in her own circle. David was on a date tonight. Carrie was on a date tonight. Sean was more than likely on a date tonight—or doing something stupid. And here she was, following David around town like some psycho stalker. But she was just protecting him, right? She just wanted to make sure nobody took advantage of him or tried to take his life.

It was the least she could do after he saved her life years ago, or so she told herself.

Veronica heard an engine roar through the parking garage below. She made sure to stay out of sight as another car entered their level, an old black station wagon. The vehicle had been modified with extra-large tires, and spikes adorned the front grill. Veronica nearly gagged on the thick exhaust the vehicle exhaled as it traveled all the way to the top of the structure and parked diagonally across a few of the spaces not too far from David and Brittany.

Veronica peered over the top of the stairwell and watched as David's eyes widened at the intrusion.

"What's going on here?" David asked.

Brittany smiled at him, flickering the ends of her skirt around playfully. "Whatever do you mean, oh hero of Anaisha."

Crap. This was about to go south quickly.

David stepped back a few feet and reached to his back pocket. The look of surprise that came over his face told Veronica that he didn't have his boomerang back there. Veronica slapped her forehead in frustration. She had told him numerous times to make sure he kept that on him at all times. If he wasn't going to fight with modern weapons, he had to at least keep the ones he would fight with on him. Especially on a blind date!

Veronica took a deep breath and waited. She would have to find the right moment to intercede. But what was she going to do without a weapon of her own?

"What's the matter, hero?" Brittany asked him as the door of the black car opened. Out of the driver's side stepped a tall man in a black leather jacket and tight jeans. He was so tall that Veronica was surprised he had even fit inside the cramped-looking station wagon.

Brittany reached into the back waistline of her skirt and pulled out David's boomerang, tossing it to the new visitor.

Veronica shook her head. So, David was prepared, just not all that alert around Little Miss Pigtails.

The tall man took the boomerang in hand and waved it at David. "The sword of Excalibur. Your weapon, isn't it?"

David didn't speak. Veronica watched his gaze dance around the structure, looking for a way of escape, for a way out of the fight. Veronica knew that wasn't what he should be thinking about though. There was no way to avoid a confrontation at this point. This was an ambush, and he should be thinking of ways to fight.

"What do you two want?"

The girl bounced up and down in her short skirt, her pigtails bouncing with her movements. She smiled a devilish grin and pointed her finger in David's face. "You. And I delivered you! Aheeheehee!"

The man smiled. "That you did, Jewels. That you did."

David sneered. "Jewels?"

She nodded, stepping toward the man in the biker's jacket. The man leaned down and kissed her, then he pinched her rear end and smacked it. "This here is my baby girl."

"What do you two want?"

The man took the boomerang and broke it over his knee, snapping it in half. "I, for one, want you dead. So does the rest of Lysallis's less-righteous community. So, as a public service, I have taken it upon myself to give the community what they want: your head on a platter."

Even from her hiding spot, Veronica could see the fear in David's eyes. "Are you crazy?"

The girl shook her head, sticking her finger in her mouth as she did it. "We're not crazy," she remarked. "We're brilliant. You fell for our little trap! Ahee hee hee hee!"

David wasn't glancing around anymore. Instead, he was sizing up the guy who had broken his only weapon. Veronica knew it was around this point that he would try to fight them off. But there were two of them and a vehicle. She wasn't sure he would win on his own, and so she resolved internally that she may be forced to reveal her presence to them and to David.

The man walked around his car and took out a cigarette, lighting it while the girl bounced up and down in front of David, apparently mocking his capture.

"Listen, David," the man said. "Lots of people want you dead right now. Now, whether I deliver you to the highest bidder or simply kill you myself and claim the bounty doesn't really matter to me." He took a puff off the cigarette and made his way back around the car toward David. "I really don't like you. I never have. You put my brother away, and I can't say that I'm all that appreciative."

David stared the man in the eyes, standing tall while he did it. "I don't really care what you are or aren't appreciative of. I'll be putting you two away while I'm here tonight and then how are you going to feel?"

Veronica shook her head. Why did David have to mouth off all the time?

The man took another puff off the cigarette, blowing the smoke into David's face. "See, I had Jewels here bring you up here tonight so I could have a nice face-to-face chat with you. But here you go again, being uncooperative and rebellious. Why can't you stop with the whole rebel attitude? It doesn't suit you."

"You're a criminal."

The man laughed, taking another puff off the cigarette. He blew the smoke out in a long cloud. "A criminal? Are you sure about that? I simply told you that you put my brother away, that doesn't mean that *I'm* a criminal. It means that maybe my brother was."

"I've already activated a tracking device that has alerted the police to my presence. If I were you, I would get out of here as fast as you can."

The girl bounced up and down again. Veronica wanted so badly to put that tramp out of her misery, but also wanted to keep the element of surprise as long as possible.

Jewels twirled around in her short, slutty skirt, "You, David Corbin, have been tricked. The only tracking device you activated was the one I switched with yours."

David grimaced. "What are you talking about?"

She pulled a black square-shaped device from inside of her bra and then waved it in his face. "This is your tracking device, stupid!"

David pulled out a device similar to hers. "Then what was this?"

"The one I traded you." Her eyes grew wide and the smile on her face lengthened, like a menacing afternoon shadow. You just alerted our gang. They should be here in a matter of minutes."

David threw the device at her face and then lunged toward her. They both fell to the cement ground of the parking structure and wrestled.

Veronica thought this might be her moment to intervene, but continued to stay put on the stairwell as she watched the guy standing by the car finish smoking his cigarette. He didn't move, but simply watched David and Jewels go at each other on the ground.

"This is entertaining. Anaisha's hero, wrestling on the ground of the parking structure with a girl about half his size."

David knocked the small device out of her hand as it bounced across the cement and landed feet from them.

The girl jabbed her nails into David's throat and pulled, cutting the skin and drawing blood. David grabbed her hands and pulled her to her feet. Then he shoved her into the smoker. His cigarette fell into the girl's cleavage and her voice came out in a shrill screech that reminded Veronica of the hornbill duckbillies at the zoo.

Veronica had to give David credit. That would keep them busy long enough to…

Sure enough, David dove for the device and started pushing the button madly.

The man with the cigarette pushed Jewels off him as she fell to the ground by the wall of the structure, screaming and brushing at her chest with wild hands. "You burned me! You burned me!"

"Shut up!" The man slapped her across the face, knocking her to the ground. Then he turned toward David who was getting to his feet. "You made a big mistake."

David lunged toward the guy, slamming him onto the hood of the station wagon. The guy wrapped his arms around David and started beating him in the back with his fists.

Veronica knew it was time to move in. She slowly stood up and was about to head toward them when something touched her shoulder and caused her to spin around in reaction.

A man stood there. He was bald, he wore a dark gray cloak over a dark-colored shirt and pants, and his eyes were a bit bloodshot. He motioned with his finger for her to keep quiet and then tried to motion for her to head back down the stairwell, out of sight. She shook her head. Something about the crooked way his finger bent or the way his lips moved like worms across his face struck dread deep inside the internal core of her being. She feared turning her back on him, but she risked a quick glance at the fiasco on the parking structure roof and watched David pop his fist into the smoker's face before getting an elbow in his own.

She turned back to the strange creature in the stairwell with her. He looked up at her from a few steps down, like a rabid animal that had exited the shadows to look for food or companionship.

"I have something that might interest you," he said, his voice deep and dark. "Something that I believe you can use."

"I suggest you get away from me."

He licked his lips. "Your friend out there is in his own battle. You cannot and should not intervene. You lack the necessary skills to protect him anyway, as much as you would like to think that you could."

"What are you talking about?"

He pointed to David. "That man that is fighting your friend already has defenses in place to fight your friend. If you intervene without your own defensive skills, strategy, or weapons, then you are a fool who does not value their life."

"That's what you think." She turned away from the strange

man, her intention to break up the fight and at least even the odds for David.

She felt the cloaked man grab her arm. "That's what I know."

She pulled her arm out of his grip and started toward David and the other guy. The girl was conscious now and a bit dazed. She leaped on David's back and started to scratch up his face, tearing into his skin with her sharp nails as she wailed like a banshee.

David moved backwards and slammed her up against the side of the car a few times. She let go of him and fell to the ground as David punched the smoker in the face again. Veronica was already halfway to them when the sound of sirens echoed in the distance. *The police!*

She spun around and dove back toward the stairwell, hoping with all of her might that David hadn't seen her. The cloaked man was still there, smiling deviously at her.

"I told you."

"Shut up," she remarked as she crouched back down at the top of the stair well. She turned back and watched David and the fight as police sirens moved up through the parking structure, drawing closer to their location. The man fled from David's grasp and bolted into his car. When he started it, the girl screamed for him not to leave without her.

David hunched over, his face a bit bloodied and beaten. He was out of breath, scratches along his neck and face. The car started and the man rolled the window down, yelling something out to David that Veronica couldn't make out. The girl dove through the side window of the car and squirmed to get herself all the way in.

Veronica let out a quiet sigh, happy that the situation was over and that David had survived. Two police cars bolted up to the top level of the parking structure, signaling that the chaos

21

was over. To her surprise, David grabbed onto the back of the man's car as it started to flee the scene. He held onto the trunk as the man drove them into one of the cop cars, tearing through part of the officer's grill before shooting down into the bowels of the parking structure.

Veronica shoved the bald man out of the way and made her way down the stairwell, knowing now that she would have to reveal her presence in order to save David's life. The bald man followed after her, lecturing her on how she needed weapons and the ability to fight before going into a battle. She would have stopped to spin around and punch him in the gut, but she knew she didn't have time. She feared touching him, as he seemed to radiate a dark, corrupted presence.

As she reached the next level of the parking structure, the car tore past her with David hanging on for dear life. She continued at a rapid pace down the stairwell, the tires of the car squealing throughout the whole structure. Her heart beat fast as she wondered why David leaped onto the car in the first place. The police were there, and they would have caught the guy...right?

She managed to make it to the next level of the parking structure before the car. She waited for a brief moment against the cement wall, catching her breath.

The vehicle roared toward her from around the corner of the structure's pillars. She debated on what to do. If she stood in the middle of the garage, he would surely run her over. Or maybe not. She took her place in the middle of the structure as the car barreled toward her.

The bald man came down the steps and shook his head. "This isn't the way to do this. I can show you an easier way, one where your friend doesn't have to get hurt. One that will enable you to protect him without compromising your principles."

She chose to ignore him. Who was he, anyway? She didn't care. She had to save David…by any means necessary. The man in the car saw her now. She closed her eyes and waited, hoping he would stop in time and enable her and David to capture him together. She felt something brush past her.

The sound of screeching tires rumbled through the structure, as if the car itself was a beast that had just been shot with a tranquilizer dart and was going down for the count. She heard metal and felt objects hit her. She fell to the ground and felt a force move her out of the way.

When Veronica opened her eyes, her vision was full of dark smoke—smoke that was pouring out of the damaged vehicle that was now halfway through one of the structure's pillars. Her heart sank into her stomach. She could hear screaming and mumbling.

She felt someone helping her up.

When she got to her feet, she realized it was the bald man. He nodded, as if he was satisfied that he had proven some point to her now. "I told you that wouldn't work."

She glanced around. "Where is David?!"

The bald man shrugged.

She looked towards the pillar and was relieved David wasn't there. The man and the girl in the car were bloodied and mumbling incoherently. She chose not to help them, though everything inside of her told her she should. They were badly hurt. They needed medical attention. But for once, she didn't care. They had almost killed David.

David stumbled out from behind a pillar a few hundred feet back from where the car had skidded out of control. He was clutching his ribs and seemed to be in a bit of pain.

Veronica rushed over to him, grabbing him in her arms as he collapsed to the ground, breathing heavily. "David? David, are you alright?"

He nodded, looking up at her through blood coating the side of his face. "I'm alright. Just a few sore ribs. What are you doing here?"

"I uh…" She had to think fast. Then she remembered the device. "I was close by and was alerted by the police when you pressed the alert button."

"Holy cow that was fast."

She nodded. "Lucky I was here, huh?"

"You were the one that stopped his car?"

She shrugged. "I knew I had to or something might have happened to you."

He started to laugh but stopped abruptly when the pain tremored through his side. "Yeah. Probably. How are they doing? Are they still alive?"

She nodded.

"We need to help them out."

She shook her head. "No, we don't."

He raised an eyebrow at her. "What do you mean we don't? They're hurt."

"Yes, but they almost killed you. That tramp and her stupid boyfriend can rot in that car for all I care."

David stared at her for a moment. Then he let the words out with some trepidation. "I'm disappointed in you, Veronica. You of all people wouldn't ever leave anyone behind like that."

"That's before people started setting up ambush plots to try and kill you."

He chuckled. "Kill me? Everyone wants to kill me, Veronica. All the time. Nothing new for me. I've learned to deal with it."

"I haven't, David." She whispered under her breath, "And I probably never will."

She helped him to his feet. When she glanced over her shoulder to look at the car, the bald man was gone.

A strange hissing moved to the forefront of the sounds playing around her. The hissing frightened her, an omen of what was about to happen.

She grabbed David and took him to the pillars he had run out from behind as the car exploded, sending a wave of heat and debris toward them. Veronica shielded David with her own body. She felt the warmth radiating from the explosion as it flowed around the pillar and engulfed her back. She felt it burn through her blouse as she cried out in anguish.

Then it was over. She fell to the ground, her back smoking. David fell to the ground too and fell unconscious. It was too much for him. As she knew it would be.

She felt the cool air of the parking structure blow across her now bare and burnt back, satisfied that she had protected him...just as she had vowed to.

CHAPTER 2

Ashes to Ashes

Her time in the small hospital bed gave Veronica a chance to think about things. A lot of things.

The man with the cigarette, and Brittany, were both still alive but in critical condition. They had accrued horrible burns to their bodies. Veronica wondered if there had actually been anything she could have done to save them from such a horrible fate.

Then again, did they deserve what happened to them?

She wrestled with this for a time. She didn't want to hurt others. But she would hurt others to protect David.

But had she been wise in following David? She felt like an idiot and a stalker for pursuing him under the guise of protecting him. Was she obsessed with him? Was there something else at the root of her insistence she keep tabs on him all the time?

David was always getting himself into trouble, this much Veronica knew. But would the entirety of the rest of her days be consumed with her watching over him at the expense of her own pursuit of love and happiness? On a Friday night when she could be engrossing herself in fashion design or attending her own blind date, she was consumed with tracking a man she gave all allegiance to. One who was always going to be in danger. One who seemed to *want* to be in danger all the time.

Veronica wrestled with her vow to protect David at all costs. The life debt she had sworn to him was her own. He knew nothing of it. In essence, she could walk away from it and only she would know of her self-betrayal.

But was it only about protecting David? Or was it also about protecting the leader of the Lazerblades? There was a higher calling buried in her vow to watch over him, but Veronica overlooked that higher calling and always focused more on the immediate tapestry that was woven: David was like a brother to her, and he had risked his life to save hers, not just at the clock tower, but on other occasions as well.

She owed him her life.

Didn't she?

At some point during her hospital stay, the bald man from the stairwell visited her. He donned the same dark cloak he had been wearing at the parking structure, but his bloodshot eyes had cleared up a bit.

She threatened to kill him if he showed his face around her again, but he assured her that he was an ally, not an enemy. Veronica knew she couldn't trust him, but she chose to listen to him anyway, if for no other reason than to evaluate the threat he posed not only to her or to David, but to society as a whole.

It was two in the morning, when David was sleeping steadily in the room next to her, that the man with the bald head properly introduced himself as Simper Creed. He explained to Veronica how he was involved in what he called dark arts. He then went on to explain what rhodenine was—a particle in Anaisha's atmosphere that had no known origin. He then told her that the ways of the dark arts allowed him to pull fragments of the strange particle out of the air and use those fragments as a powerful force against others, to bend its will to his own.

He insisted he be allowed to teach her what he knew. His reason for this was simple. She was one of Anaisha's heroes and he admired the fact that she wanted to spend the rest of her life protecting David.

After the man gave her his contact info and left, Veronica rested in the hospital bed, pondering the subject this man had brought up. Did she want to spend the rest of her life peering over David's shoulder? Is that what she wanted to do with her life?

She pondered this to the point of anxiety. She could, of course, bail out on her vow any time she wanted to. But she suddenly couldn't bear the thought of losing David. Of not giving her life to him, to protect him like she had done tonight. Granted, she almost died in the process, but she would have died years earlier if David hadn't stepped up to the plate and rescued her and Carrie from Tabitha Rose.

Walking out of the hospital with David by her side, Veronica realized she would do anything for him—well, anything that was in her power. And her power, as displayed a couple of nights earlier, had been minimal. Would it benefit her to learn this strange art that Simper Creed wanted to teach her? She turned to David, watching as he headed toward the car that Carrie had running in the loop of the hospital parking lot.

She would have to see.

***

A couple of days later, after making sure David was completely healed, and after attending to her own burns (which she had to have Carrie rub ointment on her back three times a day), Veronica decided to contact Simper Creed. She did so by phone, and he told her where he lived. She laughed when he was done giving her his home address, and then she asked him point blank how stupid he thought she was to think she would go alone to his place of residence.

He reluctantly agreed to meet her at the Jewelplex Mall.

Veronica stood in front of the sunglass shop, waiting for Simper. He arrived ten minutes late. This irritated Veronica but she let it slide. If he could teach her what he told her he could teach her, then she could protect David adequately enough. With Mr. Big still on the loose in Anaisha somewhere, she had to keep a close eye on David and all of those close to him.

"Sorry I am late," he apologized. He was dressed in the same cloak. Onlookers didn't pay him too much mind as a cloak wasn't the weirdest thing people wore in Lysallis. His eyes were bloodshot again. His demeanor seemed exhausted, worn down.

She frowned. "Whatever."

He sighed. "Where would you like to start training?"

"Here, in the mall. You think I'm going to go somewhere with you alone when I don't even know who you are?"

"I told you. I am Simper Creed." He looked genuinely confused, as if his name alone should prompt her unwavering trust in him.

"That tells me nothing. I don't trust you."

"I could say the same for you."

"You said I was one of Anaisha's heroes. How can you say you don't trust me if that's the way you truly feel about me?"

"There is a difference between having a respect for someone and trusting them."

She realized he had a point.

"We cannot train inside the mall," he said. "We will have to train outside somewhere. Maybe we can go to the courtyard, and I can show you what I can do."

She agreed. They made their way out of the nearly empty mall and to the courtyard in the front of the building. Pretty lights dangled from the feathery trees, and water pumped through the stone fountain, adding a romantic ambiance to the shopping center.

Simper examined their surroundings, apparently making sure nobody was really around to see what he was about to do. He looked at Veronica for a moment and then held his palms out in front of himself. His hands were weathered and calloused. Warts were sprinkled across his fingers, and his nails held dirt caked underneath them.

"The trick is to have full concentration." He grinned at her, but his smile did nothing to instill confidence or peace within her spirit. Instead, when he grinned, Veronica imagined a feral animal smiling before pouncing on its intended prey. "My theory is that the reaction for each individual will almost always be different depending on your bodily chemistry and the specific environment that you are in. Always try to pick an environment that would be rich in rhodenine, like the outdoors. That is why I took you out here. Less concentration on my part if we are out here as opposed to being inside of the mall."

Veronica nodded, hesitant to take the man seriously.

He closed his eyes and sat in the grass surrounding one of the trees. Then he moved his fingers around. A strange blue and purple colored light started to form in his palms. The colors were beautiful, Veronica admitted to herself. But they quickly turned black. The strange energy in the form of small balls in his palms grew larger and larger. When they were the size of his fists, Simper opened his eyes and turned toward her.

His pupils were completely black.

He smiled. His tongue was black and so were his teeth. She stood up and took a few steps away from him.

"Do not be afraid, dear Veronica. This is simply the effects of the rhodenine. A word of caution: Rhodenine can be fatal if you do not control it properly. It is a poison to the body that cannot harness its power."

She watched with horror as he thrust his palms out and sent the energy balls flying out in front of them. The projectiles hit the grass at their feet, turning the green blades black as they immediately withered and died.

"What happened?"

Simper was hunched over now, cradling his neck in his arms. "Sinter daigodus rechardim."

"What?"

He looked up at her. His eyes and mouth were back to normal.

"What the heck just happened?"

He seemed dazed. "I killed the grass with the dark art."

"What was that language you were just speaking in?"

He smiled and stood to his feet, brushing his hands off on his pants. "Let's go before anyone sees us."

Veronica grabbed his arm and stopped him in his tracks. "You're going to tell me what the heck is going on or I'm going to turn you in. How does that sound?"

He grinned. His eyes made their way down to her grip on his arm and he grinned wider at this. "If you want to touch me, fine. But I must warn you that I can strike you down in a heartbeat."

"Then why don't you? Why are you even teaching me a power this deadly?"

"Why not?"

She shook her head. "You have other motives, I can sense that much."

He pulled his arm free of her grip and walked past her. "Follow me if you want to learn more. I have your curiosity now, don't I?"

She didn't want to admit it, but he *did* have her curiosity. At the same time, she felt a strange urge to destroy him. She sensed a great evil in him. She wasn't sure if it was his power or if it was the strange language she had witnessed him speaking, but she knew deep down inside that she had to put a stop to him. The best way to do that would be to hang around him, let him train her.

Her pocket vibrated. She pulled out her cell phone and answered it, knowing it was Carrie by the caller ID.

"Veronica? Just wondering if you wanted to come to dinner tonight with David and I. We're going to go to the pizza parlor."

Veronica thought for a moment. Simper Creed stopped in front of her and shook his head. "It is essential that I train you tonight. You must stay with me, and I will continue to show you how to harness this incredible power."

Veronica knew he was right. She had an urge to learn this now. To get to know him better, if anything to simply know how to destroy him later when the time came. "Sorry. I have plans tonight."

"Plans? With who?"

"I really just want some time alone."

There was a long silence on the other end of the phone. Veronica rolled her eyes.

Carrie sighed. "Okay, I'll talk to you later."

Veronica stuck the phone in her pocket and followed Simper out to the parking lot.

"I will take you back to my house where I will continue to train you."

Veronica shook her head. "Listen, Simper Creep. I am not

going with you back to your house. Tonight isn't going to end in a one-night stand or anything like that. If you want to train, we can go to the park or somewhere else that is public. And I drove myself here, so I'm pretty sure that you can just have me follow you wherever we end up deciding to go."

He stopped before they reached the end of the courtyard. "Listen very closely to me, Veronica Amorou. I am not playing games. Whether you believe that or not is irrelevant to what I am trying to do here. I am simply trying to offer you an opportunity to help your friend."

"And you, Mr. Creed, are underestimating me. I'm not a fool. I'm not your plaything. I'm not your blind date. If you want to show me your mad skillz, then you can show them to me in public. I am one of Anaisha's heroes, right? And being so, I'm not going to be tricked into going someplace alone with you. I'm not an idiot."

Simper stared at her for a moment and then stared off toward the parking lot. She couldn't tell if he was thinking or trying to keep control of his temper.

"Fine," he finally stated. "I will train you at the top of the parking structure in downtown Lysallis, where your friend, David Corbin, was ambushed."

She nodded. "That's better."

He looked at her, his beady eyes and thin smirk speaking volumes about the derision he felt toward her. "Well, I'm so happy I could accommodate you."

"I will meet you there."

He nodded.

***

Three hours later, after sunset, they both met at the location that had been agreed upon earlier in the day. They had to park on the lower levels and sneak up to the top because one of the levels was still blocked off due to the car wreck and explosion from a week earlier.

Veronica and Simper made their way up the stairwell to the top level of the parking structure. Veronica wrestled with feelings of guilt for what happened to David's attackers. Could she have prevented their injuries? Could she have saved them from the explosion? Sure, they were alive, but could Veronica have saved them from some pain and misery?

She shook her head. She couldn't beat herself up over that stuff. She had to stay strong in her convictions. They deserved what they got. That's what she would keep telling herself. They were going to kill David that night. And if he didn't have the guts to hurt them, she would. Besides, she didn't look at it as something she did *to* them. She looked at it as they were the idiots that crashed the car. She was simply the one who put her attention on protecting David instead of trying to save them.

Once they reached the top level, Simper led her to the edge of the parking structure. She looked out at the tall blue bank building lit up in blue neon. It was beautiful, and it reminded her of David.

She regretted turning Carrie's invitation down for pizza.

Simper looked out on the city and started mumbling strange words to himself. Veronica tried to make sense of what he was saying, but the only thing she could conclude was that it was similar to the language he had spoken earlier at the mall.

"You wanna tell me what the heck that language is that you're speaking?"

He refused to look at her or stop speaking. Instead, he raised his hands up above his head, closed his eyes, and continued to mumble the words, only louder now. "Simperadum. Chronisies. Ryshum."

Veronica watched as his eyes turned black again and energy crept into his palms once more. This time though, there was a crackle in the air. She could feel an energy moving through the space where oxygen and reality combined, and it pulled the hairs up on her back and neck.

Simper turned toward her with his darkened eyes and smiled. "Watch and learn, oh hero of Anaisha." Then he twisted his arms together out in front of himself. A black beam of energy flowed out of his palms and struck the abandoned apartment building across the street. The mortar and brick shuddered under the impact as dark color splashed against the brick. The roof splintered inward, and the glass windows shattered.

Veronica watched in horror as the area tremored. Instinctively, she shoved herself into him, knocking him to the ground with a powerful blow. The beam stopped but, as she peered over the edge of the parking structure, it was too late.

The building was nothing more than a pile of ashes.

She found Simper rolling around on the ground, mumbling his strange language. She reached down and grabbed him by the collars and pulled him close to her face.

"What did you do?! I'm turning you in, you freak!"

His black teeth chattered with laughter, and his black tongue sprung in and out like a yo-yo.

He was under the influence of something horrible and Veronica wanted no part of it. She pulled out her cell phone and dialed the number to the police. After reporting the incident, she stayed there on the roof of the parking structure to make sure he didn't go anywhere.

He didn't move, except to shiver in the fetal position as he mumbled his strange language.

The police came and arrested him. Veronica told the officers she was pursuing Simper and had managed to track him to the top of the parking structure, interrupting him in the middle of his attack. The building he destroyed was known to be abandoned, but nobody could tell for sure if it had been occupied or not. All that remained of it was a mountainous pile of black ash.

***

That night, she drove home alone. The songs on the radio echoed the hurt in her heart. Had anyone died in that building tonight? How could she allow him to con her like that?

David of all people hated to see death and destruction. He wanted peace. That was all. He didn't want to use violent means to get that peace, but nobody really seemed to respect him for that. Nobody but her. And Carrie.

Veronica let herself cry on the way home that night. The darkness of the night shielded her tears from anyone's eyes. She let it all fall out and for that, she felt relieved. She felt free. She never wanted to see that evil man again. She would find ways to protect David. To keep her oath. To respect his need for peace.

She arrived home and walked into a dark and quiet house. Sean was most likely asleep. She turned on the light in her bedroom and felt relieved to be home, to be out of the hospital, to be away from that horrible man who had tried to take advantage of her tonight.

She changed into her pajamas and laid in the bed that night, staring at the ceiling, wondering about everything.

Where was Mr. Big? Was David doing okay? Did he and Carrie have fun at the pizza parlor without her?

She drifted off to sleep wondering what tomorrow would bring.

CHAPTER 3

The Ancient Ones

The next day, Veronica decided to spend some time with her friends. They had plagued her mind throughout the night, making it hard to sleep. David and Carrie had nowhere to be, so she invited them to go to the coffee shop with her. Once there, sitting down in front of her two best friends, she felt a nearly overwhelming urge to tell them everything that had happened. But she couldn't. She had to keep her secrets to herself.

David sipped some of his coffee and sighed. "Well, don't know how it happened, but some store downtown got creamed."

Carrie nodded, sipping her herbal tea. "Yeah, I heard about that on this morning's news. They don't know what it was. Some creepy looking guy was arrested and thrown in prison because of it."

"At least it wasn't Mr. Big."

Veronica nodded in agreement. *Yes, at least it wasn't Mr. Big.*

Veronica wondered where that tub of lard was. She wanted him to just show himself so they could do away with him. It was time to put an end to them always having to look over their shoulders every five minutes of the day because of him. It was time to put an end to fear. She felt the frustrations rising in her again.

David was staring at her now. Why did he have to have such an intense stare, one that could pierce through to her very core? He was the only one that could do that to her. That could have that effect on her. She hated him for it, but at the same time she loved him because of it.

"What's wrong, Veronica?"

She didn't want to open her mouth. She couldn't lie to him. She couldn't tell him the truth. She couldn't speak. She shrugged.

Now Carrie was staring at her. Her stare was a bit different. It was one of suspicion. She knew her friend like the back of her hand and Veronica hated her for it as much as she hated David for his insight into her own heart.

An explosion rocked the street outside.

The glass windows of the coffee shop shattered and blasted glass all over the patrons that were sitting close enough to them. Heat poured into the shop, and a flash of orange and red light saturated Veronica's vision momentarily as she and her friends felt the weight of the table pull them to the floor, glass crunching underneath them, screams echoing throughout the building.

Veronica got to her feet as quickly as she could muster. She helped David and Carrie stand as they all brushed glass from their clothing.

"What was that?" David asked.

Without answering the question, they rushed outside.

A nearby building had blown up. Thick, black smoke poured into the street. Carrie and David were already running toward the destruction. Veronica hesitated, wondering what could have possibly happened. She willed her legs to move and forced herself to run after her friends.

The building that had exploded was a small laundromat.

People milled about in the street, their faces flush with confusion and terror. Kids cried for their parents while car alarms rang out.

Veronica followed after David and Carrie, who seemingly vanished into the thick smoke.

Veronica managed to track them into the laundromat. As she entered the building, she quickly became disoriented. She fell to her knees, realizing she was lost in the strange haze. Her chest tightened and she coughed, her breathing coming in struggling pulses. She narrowed her eyes and peered through the smoke but couldn't find her friends—or anyone else for that matter.

"Veronica. I am disappointed in you."

She looked up and saw Simper Creed standing next to her, shrouded in his black cloak. His bald head and black eyes seemed out of place as he glared at her. She felt her lungs tighten, and knew it was him who was squeezing the life out of her, but she did not know how.

"I will keep squeezing until you agree to follow me and my ways. It's important you learn what I know because David will need your assistance up ahead. I know this because I was told. I was told by the Ancient Ones."

"Ancient ones?"

He nodded, reaching his hand out to her. She refused. Then she felt her lungs squeeze tighter together, suffocating her.

"I made this explosion. I created this destruction so I could get you alone. You're always with your friends. I want to be your friend too."

She shook her head. "You...You are no...friend...of..."

"Don't say it!"

She felt her airway seal up. He was going to kill her now. She fell to the ground, the asphalt scraping her cheek.

"I won't hesitate to kill you, Veronica. But I won't today. I

39

need you. And you need me."

She felt the smoke getting darker now, and she closed her eyes. She wondered if David and Carrie were walking into a trap. She wondered if she would ever wake up.

***

Veronica's eyes fluttered open. Through hazy memories and blurry vision, she fought panic. She wasn't at home in her bed. She wasn't at home at all. As her vision cleared, she found herself in a strange bedroom decorated in black furniture. The bed she was laying in was soft and comfortable. Peering under the covers, she realized she was still in the clothes she had been wearing the day she had coffee with her friends—jeans and a purple blouse.

Where were her friends?

She slowly sat up, her head pounding. She glanced over to a small digital clock on the nightstand. It was ten at night. Had she only been here for the day? Where was she?

Deep inside her gut, she knew where she was. She was in Simper Creed's home.

Veronica swung her legs over the edge of the bed and made contact with the carpet. Her bare feet felt the warmth of the fibers, and this relaxed the pounding in her head a bit. She slowly stood to her feet and walked to the bedroom door, which was cracked open an inch. The hallway was filled with darkness, save for a bluish light at the very end of the corridor. A strange smell permeated the house, but she couldn't pinpoint it. A mixture of herbs and incense maybe.

She stepped into the hallway and started toward the end of it, her senses awake and aware of her surroundings. The house was two stories, at least. It was raining outside. The heater ran, but a cold chill lingered in the air of the hallway. The carpet felt moist under her feet, but she ignored that fact and drew closer to the end of the corridor.

How could she have been so weak and stupid to allow herself to be captured by this madman? Where were her friends? Did David and Carrie know where she was? That she had been taken?

There were pictures on the wall, but she couldn't make them out due to the lack of light. She didn't want to make them out. She wanted to regain her strength and fight with every fiber of her being to get out of this nightmare. This time she would make sure Simper was locked up in solitary confinement until the end of his days.

She reached the source of the blue light: an office that smelled of leather. Soft blue lighting poured from the ceiling. Tall bookshelves covered the walls, and a large desk sat on the other side of the room.

Simper was sitting there, spectacles on, scouring papers. "I see you have awoken. I hope your headache gets better. Should be gone in an hour or so."

Her head indeed screamed at her for even attempting to move from the bed.

"It's the effects of the suffocation. I simply needed to knock you unconscious."

"I'll kill you."

He looked up at her, pushing his papers to the side. Then he took his glasses off and folded them up, his hands looking mammoth with the thin wire frames in their grip. "You won't. You can't. You are weak, Veronica. You and your friends together are a force to be reckoned with. But alone, you are weak. You have no superpowers. You have no real weapons. When you and your friends are together, though, you have the ability to get things done. But you won't always have your friends. I need you to learn this lesson above all others. I need you to trust me that I want the very best for you and even for your friends."

She breathed through clenched teeth. "I already told you that I don't trust you."

He stood up and set his spectacles on the desk. His dark cloak made him look somewhat monk-like, but she knew of the villainy and chaos that the cloak hid. "I am very sorry that you feel that way. But you will have a change of heart and a change of mind very soon. I have a few things to show you. If you do not wish to stay here after I show you those things, then I will leave you alone until the end of time. I promise."

Veronica couldn't help but chuckle. She stumbled a bit and tripped, hitting the floor with her elbows. She cursed under her breath, and her head scolded her by revealing the beginnings of a migraine. "You promise?" she asked sarcastically.

He nodded as he stepped out from behind the desk. "I do promise. My word is my word. I know you may not have liked what you saw back in Lysallis, but it was necessary to show you a real-world example of the power that can be at your disposal if you will just allow it to become a part of you. If you will allow me to train you."

"I don't believe this. I don't believe that you want what's best for me. I don't believe you have a true heart. I don't believe anything you say."

He shrugged. "Doesn't really matter, does it? You are trapped here until you see what I want to show you. It's all up to you."

She seethed. "I will kill you."

He shook his head. "Like I said before, you are too weak to kill me." He held his hand out for her to take. She hesitated for a few moments, and then took it. He pulled her to her feet and then stared at her, those beady black eyes missing a soul behind them.

She fought the urge to claw his face off. "What are you looking at?"

"I am looking at a beautiful woman who can do miraculous things. You just have to believe in yourself." He reached his hands to her face. She flinched. He moved her hair to the sides around her ears and then cupped her chin in his palm. "You are so gorgeous, Veronica. Why nobody has seen that yet is a mystery to me."

She swung her arm in front of her and knocked his hand away from her. "Get away from me. You touch me again, I'll snap your arm in two."

He smiled. "That's the spirit. You have it inside of you, but you refuse to release it." He motioned for her to follow him. She did so, following his trail as it snaked through the large house. Apparently, her room was only a small guest room compared to the rest of his fortress. They made their way downstairs via a massive spiraling staircase, and then passed through a spacious kitchen, complete with pizza oven and spice room.

He led them through a back door that exited off the kitchen into a massive yard filled with a garden live with beautiful winter-born plants and flowers.

"Where did you get all of the money for this place?"

He smiled. "I am glad you like your new home."

She gnashed her teeth. "This isn't my home. I wouldn't be caught dead living here with you."

"It doesn't matter where I get my money. I have it, and if you aren't related to me in any manner, then it is none of your business."

She laughed inside. One minute he was trying to own her and the next he became defensive when she asked him a simple question.

He led her through the garden, which she admitted was beautiful. Rose bushes surrounded her, and sprinkled between them were cherry blossom trees, their lengthy branches arching overhead with the buds of what would soon blossom when spring came around. She took a deep breath and breathed in the exotic scents. They put her mind at ease, and she felt her body relax a bit.

They stopped in the middle of the garden and Simper turned and just stared at her for a moment.

Veronica reminded herself that she would have to play his little game for just a little longer, until she was at full strength and could defeat him on her own. She couldn't bring her friends into this right now. There would be too many questions and she would have to hear too many lectures. Especially from Carrie.

"What are you staring at me for?"

"Don't you feel that?"

She took a step back, wondering what he was referring to. But then she realized that she did feel somewhat strange. Her body was continuing to relax, her nerves were beginning to loosen up. She felt the soft, massaging buzz course through her arms and legs, down her back, along her spine and neck. The strange feeling in her thighs moved into the center of her legs and the erotic feeling increased from there. It was as if there was a strange ointment down there, working some magic she had never known. She felt the strange feeling in her breasts now as well, along with the small of her neck.

Her chest tightened and her breath deepened. She felt giddy with the erotic feeling but tried to keep her mind above it. He was playing some kind of trick on her.

He nodded, motioning for her to follow him. Then he answered her, as if he knew what she was assuming. "It is not a trick. It is a treasure." He stopped in front of a small bush that was dotted with deep red flowers that had yellow circles in the center of their petals. "This is an Eros plant, named for the effects it can cast into the air around itself."

"Eros?" She tried to overpower the intense reaction her body was having to the strange plant. She felt her senses dulling somewhat. Her head felt hazy. Her skin pricked and the sensation of lost circulation filled her legs and arms.

She stepped away from the plant, shaking her head. The effects lessened, and she felt coherency return.

He folded his hands in front of himself and smiled at her. "Do not worry. I have no need for you sexually, and so I would never take advantage of you."

She stared at the Eros flowers. "Then why have these plants?"

He motioned for her to follow him further through the garden.

She followed. The further she got from the Eros plants, the clearer her thinking became. The plants, she concluded, were incredibly dangerous. The implications of what those flowers could do to others raced through Veronica's mind, and she realized, with some horror, that Simper wasn't a normal criminal. He wasn't just a crazed psychopath.

He was someone who had to be stopped.

"I have the plants because I am a botanist and a collector of fine fern life from around Anaisha."

You're a creep, and I'm going to put you down the first chance I get.

He led her to a small shed at the other end of the backyard, past garden. He used a key and unlocked the door to the building and motioned for her to step in.

She shook her head. "How stupid do I look to you?"

"My dear, if I wanted to trick you, I wouldn't have told you about the flowers. And when you walked through the flowers, I would have had my way with you. You wouldn't have been able to stop me, you would have felt too good and would have let it happen. I mean you no immediate harm. I simply want to show you some things that might peak your interest about why I brought you here."

She shook her head and crossed her arms. "You first."

He shrugged, sighed, and walked into the room, flipping on the light switch as he entered. She slowly followed suit, making sure to keep the door open for a quick escape if it was needed.

She was surprised to find four gray walls with bulletin boards on them, all covered in papers and newspaper clippings and photos of various things.

He noticed her surprise. "I've been studying Anaisha for the Ancient Ones—the gods of this planet who ruled here long ago."

"Gods?"

"Immortal beings that have infinite power. They once ruled Anaisha, as they did all of the planets in existence. We were made to serve them, but over the centuries, we as humans turned away from them and decided to serve ourselves. You can thank the Anaishan government for some of that, but ultimately, it has been our own selfish wills that have destroyed the relationship between us and our creators."

She walked around the room, keeping in mind that the door was still open for a quick escape. She marveled at all of the strange stories that were posted. Earthquakes and floods, natural disasters of all sorts. There were murders and rapes, conspiracies and robberies. She had only heard of a few of these events. Most seemed to have occurred elsewhere in Anaisha, where her knowledge did not extend.

"These things that have been happening to our world are because the Ancient Ones are furious with us and are on the brink of destroying the human race as a whole."

She did everything in her power not to roll her eyes at him.

"I know you think I'm crazy, but I assure you that I am not. The Ancient Ones have entrusted me with a mission: to find the worthiest individuals on this planet and train them to use the magic that they themselves trained me to use."

"You're telling me that these Ancient Ones taught you how to do what you did back on the street, where you choked me without touching me? Where you vaporized a building into ash? And you are so incredibly adamant to teach *me* these skills?"

He nodded.

"You're out of your mind." She started toward the open door.

He shook his head and thrust his hand out. The door slammed shut in front of her. She heard a latch slide into place. Her heart raced, but she calmed herself, realizing she was comfortable with killing this man now.

"If you choose to keep me captive here, I will do everything in my power to make sure you pay for it."

He smiled. "I encourage you to."

"Excuse me?"

Simper began pacing the room, staring at the floor with his hands behind his back as he did so. "My dear, dear child. You have so much potential that gets wasted with that little group of yours."

"The Lazerblades?"

He nodded and then looked at her. "I have wanted to tap into your power for so long now but have only recently had the opportunity to show you what I am capable of. I want to *share* my power with you, the same power the Ancient Ones gave me."

"I don't want anything to do with your power, Simper. I want to go home."

"What if I wasn't a kind man? What if I *wanted* to hurt you? To rape you, to beat you? Would you be able to defend yourself against me?"

Her pulse raced, her mind thinking of ways to defend herself, to hurt him.

He shook his head. "I don't want anything to do with harming you. If I did, I would have restrained you and killed you when you were unconscious in the street. But I didn't. I brought you into my home.

"I am willing to teach you everything I know."

"I saw you destroy a building full of people."

He shrugged. "Not really. That city building was abandoned. If there were people there, then they weren't supposed to be there. Whose fault would that be then?"

She glared at him, her fight-or-flight response going back and forth in her spirit. This man needed to be stopped, but was she powerful enough to do so?

He shook his head. "I didn't kill anyone, Veronica. There was no one in there and I knew that before I did what I did. I am not a monster. I am one who wants to pave a new path for the human race. One who does not want to face the wrath of the Ancient Ones. I want to show them that I am worthy of the life I have been given. I want to show them that not all of us humans are worthless."

Simper closed his eyes and reached his hand out, palm up. A small orb of energy began to form. He opened his eyes and brought it close to her. It was black, like the orb he had used to destroy the building back in downtown Lysallis. "This is what I can do. This orb is pure energy, pulled out of the atmosphere surrounding Anaisha. I can destroy an entire building with this alone."

She marveled at the orb now that she was closer to it. "Where did you learn to do this?"

"One of the Ancient Ones came down from his heavenly

realm and taught it to me. As I will teach it to you…if you will allow me. Think about it, Veronica. You could protect David and Carrie and your brother, Sean. You can defeat Anaisha's greatest villains. This power could be yours."

"To defend, right? Or are you planning on teaching me this so I can go on a rampage throughout the city and destroy everything and everyone in sight?"

He laughed, expelling the orb by crushing it into his palm. "I give you the freedom to decide what you want to do with this power. I will simply teach it to you."

She thought about it for a moment. She would be able to protect David, no matter what came their way. She would be unstoppable, if that's what she wanted to be…which it wasn't. She would use this to defend, that is all. She nodded to this strange man. "Fine. But if I get even the hint that you're up to something nefarious with all of this, I will cut you down with my bare hands."

He smirked. "You could not. But do not fret, I am not up to no good. I have only your best interests and the interests of the Ancient Ones in mind."

That's what I'm worried about. These Ancient Ones sound like creatures out of a horrible fairy tale.

"I would much like you to meet these Ancient Ones sometime, as I have."

"How is that even possible?"

He smiled. "It will be. One day. I will speak to them in the next week and see if they would like to meet you."

***

Veronica went home that night. She contacted Carrie and David and let them know she was alright, that she had simply gotten misplaced from her friends during the aftermath of the explosion. Carrie took what Veronica said at face value and told her that the police couldn't figure out what had happened at the laundromat. David seemed (naturally) skeptical of Veronica's story, but he didn't press her on it. Sean was still out gallivanting around town with his girlfriend, or so Veronica chose to assume.

She made her way to her own bedroom, her mind and body exhausted.

The four-post bed was there, waiting for her, calling out for her to sleep within its protective realm. To get lost in it. To put this day behind her.

She unbuttoned her blouse, letting it slide down her arms and to the floor with no sound. Then she unbuttoned her jeans and slipped off her shoes. There in the room, in only her underwear and bra, she stood, allowing the cool breeze from the night air outside her window to coast across her bare skin.

She pondered about the strange plant Simper had in his garden. The Eros. A plant that had that kind of influence over someone—especially a woman—was deadly and posed incredible danger. She knew this. And with this knowledge, she also knew it had to be investigated further.

Veronica nodded to herself in the mirror, resolving to follow Simper's instructions, if for no other reason than to keep an eye on him and find out what his plans were not just regarding the Ancient Ones, but also those twisted plants.

She slid her body across the top of the mattress comforter, feeling the cold chill of the blankets press against her skin. She wanted someone to hold her, to warm her on cold nights such as this. She wanted to feel their hands skating across her skin and their warm lips kissing hers. She slipped under the covers and lay there, staring at the mesh canopy above her bed.

A question entered her mind, and she struggled with it, wrestled with it, until she could do so no more, and the question became an addition to the collection of other questions piling up in her mind's eye.

Was she secretly in love with David?

She had skated around the issue so much because she knew that David was in love with Carrie and Carrie was in love with David. But neither of them were ever going to do anything about it. It was craziness. And at the same time, both of them were restraining themselves from real relationships.

Was she in love with David? Just as a brother…right? He was Anaisha's greatest hero. He saved her life that day in the clock tower so many years ago. Is that why she felt she loved him? Or did she feel warm and safe around David? Was she willing to die for him?

She bit her lower lip and turned on her side, closing her eyes. The thought of him made her warm. She fell asleep, thinking about him, thinking about what she felt for him…

CHAPTER 4

Training Days

The next day, Veronica headed back to Simper's home, driving through mid-morning traffic with the radio blaring jazz tunes. She was still tired and somewhat exhausted, but she also had a new resolve to stop Simper in whatever he was up to.

She had to fight the urge to call the police—or her friends—and have them raid his place of residence. Veronica knew there had to be more going on there than she was seeing, but she figured the only way she would find out what Simper was up to was to infiltrate his place, gain his trust, and manipulate his undoing.

Simper was a crafty, albeit psychotic, individual. Veronica had met others like him in the past, but there was something especially dark about him. She didn't believe all of his talk about the Ancient Ones, but she did believe that he was convinced there was a race of gods that had some sway over the people of Anaisha.

Veronica made sure to carry a small pocketknife on her, just in case the man tried anything. It wasn't a tool to be used to defend herself, not really, but it was more to be used to infiltrate or escape. It had a lockpick built into it, and she had been practicing for months picking locks just in case situations required this particular set of skills.

Veronica pulled her car into the driveway of Simper's home. The place radiated a dark presence, and she suddenly felt sick to her stomach. She sat in the car, staring at the dark brown hue of the garage door and took deep breaths to calm and collect herself.

She reminded herself to keep her wits about her around that garden. Those Eros plants would be the end of her if she wasn't careful. For all she knew, Simper's plan was to get her tangled in those things so he could have his way with her.

Veronica left the car and walked up the cement pathway to the house.

Simper greeted her at the door in his black cloak, his bald head shiny with some kind of ointment or lotion. "Today, we learn meditation."

He led her to the garden, and then to the small building located at the other end of it. Instead of unlocking the door that led to the room with the newspaper articles all over its walls, he took her to a smaller room to the side of it. This door didn't have a lock, and when she cautiously stepped inside, she found the walls were decorated in red velvet. The floor was crafted from a soft, black substance that gave a little bit of a bounce when she walked across it. Plump red and white cushions were scattered everywhere. The scent of vanilla permeated the small space.

She wondered what kind of strange activities he performed in this room.

Simper left the door open and motioned for her to sit on one of the larger pillows that had been set on the floor. She sat cross-legged, her senses wide awake to this strange place. The room had all the trappings of a place one could be ambushed in. It screamed serenity, but Veronica wasn't buying Simper's altruistic façade.

Simper walked to the front of the room and positioned himself between two small tables that each held sticks of incense. He lit the rods, and the smell of vanilla and patchouli filled the space between them.

"Meditation is important if you want to perfect the skills I am going to teach you. You must be focused. You have to be attentive to everything around you and nothing around you at the same time."

He bowed to her and then showed her the stance to take: knees on the ground, eyes closed, hands folded in front of oneself.

Veronica mimicked his motions, leaning her knees on the soft pillow.

Simper then proceeded to teach her meditation.

Hours passed, during which Veronica was taught how to drown out all outside noises, while also learning to focus on each and every one of her surroundings. She learned to hear the wildlife outside in the garden, birds, butterflies, and bees. She learned to taste the moisture in the air around them, a cold morning full of frost. She inhaled the various scents within her environment, including the strong incense, but also the faint hints of the oils Simper used on his bald scalp, the cheap laundry detergent he washed his disgusting cloak in, and the hints of the Eros plant which lay just outside their little training area—they carried a faint menthol scent. She was able to focus the status of her own body. She needed to shave her legs. She had trouble breathing out of her right nostril. And one of her breasts was indeed slightly lopsided compared to the other one. It was her right one.

Even though these facts were minute, she was proud of herself for being able to acclimate to this new way of awareness.

Veronica easily learned the meditation skills Simper taught, but her mind, her body, remained uneasy the entire time. The very thought of them being alone in that room and Simper being so close to her unnerved her.

He noticed and made a few comments here and there about her needing to relax.

She refused. She reminded herself that she wasn't here to relax. She was here to get to the bottom of Simper's agenda, unravel it, and destroy it. Maybe she could learn how to harness rhodenine in the process so she could protect her friends more aptly, but if not, she would be happy with just being responsible for Simper's undoing.

She asked herself if she would be willing to kill this man. There was something dark residing within him, but she couldn't quite piece together the whole picture yet. He was unhinged, but there were other forces working as well. Maybe there was more to the Ancient Ones that he kept mentioning.

Veronica couldn't shake the feeling that this property was being used for something wrong.

During her meditation practice, she swore she heard a soft, mewling sound. A low whine, almost a cry. The sounds would arise faintly in the background of her other focused sounds and smells, but when she tried to move her focus to the uncanny noises, they would disappear. She told herself they were figments of her imagination, but even she couldn't believe that lie.

Happy with her progress, Simper sent her home that evening without much more talk or interaction, simply agreeing to have her come back tomorrow.

***

The next day, Veronica returned to Simper's home. He answered the door in his cloak, brought her back to the room off the garden, and continued to teach her about meditation, albeit a more advanced form than the day before.

Instead of focusing on the physical—sights, sound, smells—he taught her how to dive within herself and explore the core of her being: her emotional structure.

She hesitated diving this deeply into her own subconscious at first, for fear he would use her lack of environmental awareness to do something malevolent. But once she figured out how to both delve into her inner being while also remaining aware of her surroundings, she relaxed and felt more eager and willing to explore the complicated network of feelings she had weaving their way within her.

She realized a great many things through this practice.

She did have feelings for David. She did love him, more than a brother. It wasn't information that was all that surprising to her, but it was information that she would have to keep to herself.

She found she had a great inner warmth toward Carrie. The girl was a sister to her, and Veronica would protect Carrie with her own life, much like she would do for David. However, she found Carrie to be a bit too much like the typical damsel-in-distress, always having to be rescued by David. Maybe it was intentional on Carrie's part. Maybe she *wanted* David to continually rescue her.

It was a novel thought, but Veronica didn't spend much time on it. She continued to explore her feelings, diving deep into the resentment she had for her brother, Sean. He did very little to contribute to the success of the Lazerblades, always seemed to be missing-in-action, and treated Veronica like she was a younger sister to him rather than a twin.

She dismissed most of those feelings as normal feelings that siblings shared for one another. She didn't hate Sean. Quite the opposite, really. She had a degree of respect for him, as he had to continuously put aside his own pride and ambitions to allow David to lead their group. He had a massive resentment toward David—mainly his authority and leadership—but Veronica told herself he would grow out of it as their team grew stronger, closer, and started to really make a change in the city by finally stopping Mr. Big.

At the end of this second day of training, Simper invited Veronica to have dinner with him in the main house. She reluctantly agreed. The meditation exercises were good, but she needed to dive deeper into her investigation into Simper and his motives and agenda.

Over a meal of pasta and salad, Veronica and Simper discussed her training. Simper seemed pleased with her progress but explained that this was only the beginning. He told her she would have to learn to put herself to the side to allow the power of the Ancient Ones in. She didn't believe these Ancient Ones existed at all, but she played along with it. She figured it was a form of magic or could be proven by scientific theory, not superstitious mumbo jumbo. The gods of Anaisha were all fake, she knew this much. She figured they were invented by the government to give people something to grasp in their moments of sadness and despair. And if *they* were fake, so were these Ancient Ones.

Simper explained to her that it would probably take them weeks to train. She grew irritated at this. She wanted to put an end to this charade and an end to this evil man. He was up to something, but until she found out what it was and put a stop to it, she wouldn't be free to return to her normal life.

As hard as she tried to keep her impatience hidden from Simper, he noticed, but chose to say nothing about it. Veronica figured he probably had his own issues trusting her, but he seemed incredibly confident that she was going to use the skills he taught her to benefit him somehow.

That night, after dinner, Veronica went home with a new resolve. She couldn't sit here and let this process take weeks and months to materialize. She had to fast track this, if not just to put a stop to Simper, but so she wouldn't have to explain these things to her friends.

If David found out about Simper, she was sure he might actually kill the man. Carrie would probably question Veronica's strategy of getting so close to this deranged monster. Sean...well, Veronica couldn't guess what Sean would do. He might kill Simper before David could even get to the man.

Veronica felt—knew—there was more here to be uncovered. Something larger that was being hidden. Simper was a mask on something more malevolent.

When Veronica arrived home that night, it was to an empty house again. She settled into her pajama set and sat at the worn desk in her bedroom to peruse the internet.

She searched for Simper in the search engine. As expected, nothing came from that, but she realized it was because Simper Creed was most likely a false name he used.

She put his address into the search field in the hopes something would come up, that some history would be revealed about his property.

This time she was in luck.

The search engine provided an article that went into detail about the residence, specifically about a woman named Gloria Devine who used to live there. She had been a well-known wealthy aristocrat, one of the richest people in the city of Lysallis at the time. She became involved in archaeology in her youth—something to do with ancient artifacts from Anaisha's past.

The article mentioned Gloria's obsession regarding god-like beings called Ancient Ones. *So, it wasn't just Simper!* The woman had dedicated all the days of her youth in search of some strange artifacts that held the power of the Ancient Ones—weapons, from what Veronica could discern from the way the article hinted at 'powerful artifacts.'

Unfortunately, the article didn't go into further detail.

Veronica typed 'Ancient Ones' in the search engine, but nothing—except for the article—came up. This was strange. She didn't by any means believe in any Ancient Ones. She figured it was just some superstitious nonsense. But now she knew there was a connection between the previous owner of the house and Simper. The Ancient Ones seemed to be tying them both together.

She searched Gloria's name in the search engine. She found the woman's obituary. Gloria had died less than a year ago, meaning Simper hadn't lived there for very long, unless he had some relational connection to the woman or had lived there with her. *Was she his grandmother or just the previous occupant of the house he now lived in?*

Veronica shut the computer down and turned into her bed. The day had been long, but she was even more intent now in her mission to get to the bottom of Simper and his agenda.

She drifted to sleep dreaming of massive beings that traversed time and space but held dominion in neither.

She dreamed of her and David sharing a kiss.

She dreamed of her friendship with Carrie ending.

CHAPTER 5

Controllable Urges

The days passed.

Veronica trained with Simper more, perfecting her meditation skills. She focused most of her personal training on trying to identify the mewling sounds that appeared just outside her point of focus when she was deep in meditation. But to her utter frustration, every time she tried to hone her focus on these sounds, they vanished, like vapors on the wind.

Her training with Simper did not go unnoticed by her friends. Veronica had to lie to each one of them about what she was doing. She put together a weak story about how she had started working out to get into physical shape for the missions up ahead.

This lazily tied-together story presented all sorts of problems, but it was the best Veronica could come up with. Her focus was shifted squarely toward Simper.

David didn't buy her excuse, but he left her alone. He seemed to be dealing with his own personal issues.

Carrie asked if she could join Veronica in her quest for physical fitness, as she herself needed more physical training.

Veronica kindly rejected the request and stated that this was something she had to do by herself. This only made Carrie more suspicious and hurt that her friend wouldn't want to share this part of her life with her.

Sean finally popped up at home one night, but only said he had been spending the night with a friend. Because of his own questionable absence, he didn't seem to want to question Veronica regarding hers.

Veronica's parents finally returned home from their trip but knew nothing and questioned nothing about Veronica's daily activities.

For the most part, Veronica was able to keep up her charade. But she didn't like it. She didn't like having to lie to her friends. She didn't like having to sneak around.

She didn't like Simper.

By the end of the week, Veronica was tired of training in meditation. Her efforts to figure out what the deal was with the mewling went nowhere, and she had grown increasingly tired of exploring her own feelings about things.

The last day of the week, she arrived at Simper's home and, to her surprise, he told her they were going to learn how to pull the dark power out of Anaisha's atmosphere.

They moved to the garden, and Veronica reminded herself of the Eros plants. The very last thing she could do was allow those plants to affect her. She made a mental note to research the plants online this evening. If the plants themselves had such an erotic effect just sitting in the ground, then what kind of effect would they have if they were crushed into a concoction of some type? Could it be possible that Simper was using them as some kind of date rape drug? Or maybe he just wanted to see the effects the plants had on unsuspecting women that came to his place of residence.

Simper crafted a black orb in his palm, then asked her to touch it. Veronica was hesitant at first, knowing what the orb had done to the building in Lysallis. She realized though, that Simper was able to hold the orb in his own hand, against his own flesh. By all logic, she should be able to do the same.

Simper saw her hesitation and smiled. "The energy contained in the orb is an explosive energy. It won't hurt you if you touch it, but it will if I were to propel it toward you. That's why the building was torn apart like it was."

She understood his logic and took a chance, touching the top of the orb with two fingers. The energy buzzed the tips of her fingers but otherwise didn't harm her at all. She smiled. "This is incredible."

Simper's beady eyes searched their surroundings. "This energy is all around us, Veronica. It is in the very air that we breathe."

"It must not be toxic then?"

He shook his head. "I believe it is in some individuals, but to the major populace, it is like the oxygen you breathe. Dust from the gods, as I like to call it."

"Dust from the gods, huh?"

He nodded, motioning for her to take the orb from his palm. "You can grab it with your own hand and take it from me and use it as your own. This will be your first task."

She cupped her palm over the small globe of energy and grasped it, picking it up. She turned her palm over and held the orb in front of herself. She was amazed at this strange miracle she was performing.

"Now," he said, "thrust it out toward that rose bush over there." He pointed into the distance.

She felt the energy buzzing in her palm and smiled with some degree of confidence. Then she thrust her hand out and tossed the orb toward the rose bush. The energy coasted into the bush and vaporized it to nothingness. "Whoah."

Simper smiled. "When we are talking about inanimate objects, such as nature or stone, the energy seems to disintegrate them. When it comes to humans though...well..."

She realized with some dread that he was speaking as if he had tested this theory on humans before. She suddenly became aware of her surroundings and realized she was within proximity of a bush with red flowers—the Eros flowers.

She turned to leave the garden in the direction of the house when Simper stepped in her way. "Why do you still not trust me?"

"What are you talking about?"

"You fear the flowers, yet we aren't close enough to them for you to have any type of reaction to them."

"How do you know so much about this energy you're able to call forth?"

"You mean how do I know its effects on humans?"

She nodded, still aware of the flowers. The last thing she needed was to fall into a trap of that sort. She glanced down at her watch and realized it was getting much too late. Dinnertime had fast approached. She was hungry. Tired. And she wanted to continue her research at home in the safety of her own bedroom.

"I tested this strange energy on a colleague of mine," Simper said. "He was a brilliant man but was too concerned with following rules and procedures to really want to risk the process of discovery. We both found out about this energy, and instead of wanting to test it to see how we could use it to help humanity, he wanted to study it to find out where it came from. I tried to explain to him that the gods, the Ancient Ones, had spoken to me in dreams and told me it was from them, a gift to me and my colleague for being so concerned with taking humanity to the next level of evolution.

"This friend of mine…"

Veronica watched Simper as a glazed film fell over his eyes.

"I needed a human guinea pig. So, when we were out in the fields one day, testing out some theories on where the energy matter comes from—since he didn't believe me about the Ancient Ones—I thrust an energy orb at him. I didn't want to kill him, Veronica, but I had to see what the effect of this energy was on the human body. I am one of the few on this planet that knows about this. I am one of the few that can experiment with it."

"Why didn't you try it on an animal?"

He nodded. "I did. It hurt the animal, but didn't cause it to disintegrate, like what you saw happen with the rose bush."

"What happened to your friend?"

"He was hurt, but not beyond healing. He eventually healed from the impact of the energy, but after that he left my circle and vowed never to work with me again." He had a thoughtful expression on his face, as if he was genuinely sad about the loss of his friendship with this unknown man.

Veronica wanted to ask who this colleague of his was but realized it didn't really matter.

Simper smiled at her. "That's enough for today, Veronica. Go home and get some sleep."

She agreed. She made her way off his property and returned home, pondering the story he had shared with her. He had left out important details—details that created suspicion in her. Why was it that only Simper Creed seemed to know about these Ancient Ones, let alone have dreams from them? Who was this other colleague of his? At first, she didn't think that was an important fact, but now, putting together the fact that this must have been another scientist of some type, she realized it was a relevant piece of information. Who were they and why had they just walked away from Simper Creed?

One other question that rolled around in her head was about those infernal Eros plants in Simper's garden. What was the purpose of having them there?

She would have to pry more, maybe around the house itself.

Veronica returned home and lay in bed, her mind wide awake with stirrings of Simper Creed, the Ancient Ones, and whatever the near future held for her.

***

The next day, Veronica arrived at Simper's house early for her training. She wanted to make full use of the day in the hopes of grabbing a moment or two to peruse the rest of the property. Simper was nothing if not secretive, and Veronica knew deep in her gut that something was off about not only him, but the property itself.

Against her better judgment, she wore a short black skirt and white blouse. It was juvenile to try to use seduction on a man as disgusting as Simper, but Veronica wanted to hurry this whole thing along. Her friends were no doubt suspicious about her activities, her parents would start asking questions soon enough even though they weren't home to scrutinize her comings and goings, and she really wanted nothing more to do with this foul human being.

So seduction—at least in a visual form—would have to do. She needed to search the house today. She needed answers. Was Simper some kind of mastermind that she would need her friends to stop? Or was he a mere deranged individual that the cops—and the mental institution—would need to pick up?

When she arrived at his house, he opened the door and narrowed his eyes on her. "What are you doing here so early?"

She shrugged. "I have nothing else to do. Might as well train as much as I can while I have the time, right? Why? Do you have something else to do today?"

He shook his head, his eyes drinking in her form in the short skirt and blouse. It made her feel disgusting, but she gently nudged her way past him into the house.

"Very well. Follow me outside to the garden and we will begin today's training."

"I actually need to use the restroom first." She grinned shyly. "Girl issues, know what I mean?"

His gaze changed from aroused to disgusted. "Very well. Up the stairs, to the right, third door on the left."

She nodded and headed up the flight of stairs. She could feel his gaze on her as she traveled up each ornate step. She fought the urge to tug at the end of her skirt. It was a piece of clothing she had purchased last summer. It was too short, and she meant to return it but never got around to doing so.

She reached the top of the stairs and turned to the right, wondering how much time she would have before he became even more suspicious. She made it to the third room on the left and opened the door, then shut it without going inside. She wanted to see if he would bother following her up there, but after a few seconds, she realized he must have headed outside or to somewhere else in the house.

She continued down the hallway, investigating each door of each room, trying to see if anything stood out in her mind. She wanted to find something, something that the old woman, Gloria Devine, would have left behind or something that Veronica could use to reveal Simper's mysterious shroud.

She found a strange door, black in color while the rest were white. It had an ornate looking silver doorknob on it and had strange decorative etchings around the middle part of the door itself, very elegant looking, with swirls and fancy flourishes. She reached her hand out to the knob and grabbed it. It was ice cold in her hand—so cold that she had to pull away for a moment before grabbing it again. She tried to turn it, but it wouldn't budge.

Must be locked.

She gazed closer at the surface of the door and realized there were other etchings in it besides the decorative lines. Strange symbols flanked the door frame. One was circular with an X in the middle. Another was a pinwheel design. The last was a triangle with a dot on the outer edge of each side. They were equally spaced apart from each other by a few inches and the symbols seemed to repeat themselves every three.

She heard footsteps and rushed back to the bathroom, opening the door and swiftly shutting it quietly. She darted to the toilet and flushed it, then ran the water for a moment.

What were those strange symbols? Why was the door black? She realized she had no answers, only more mysteries to what lay inside of this house and what the connection to Gloria Devine and Simper Creed was.

She opened the door and found Simper, standing, waiting for her.

"Hey."

He smiled. "I thought I heard something out of the ordinary."

She shrugged. "Not sure what you mean." She tugged at the end of her skirt, wishing it was at least a couple of inches longer. "I was in the bathroom."

"Of course you were. But I heard something strange up here. The voices of the Ancient Ones called out to me and told me to come up here."

She shuddered at his words. He really believed he was receiving instructions from these crazy ancient gods.

His eyes narrowed on her, studying her, not as someone fawning over another sexually, but the way a scientist studies the subject of their research. "What do you suppose it was that I heard? Or why I was called up here?"

She shrugged as she made her way past him and started down the stairs. "Maybe you heard me opening my tampon." Even she cringed at the mere mention of her female unmentionables. "Who knows."

He followed her as they both exited the house and entered the garden outside.

"Today, I want to teach you the to harness the very power of the Ancient Ones yourself…without my assistance." He led them through the garden, within proximity of the Eros shrubs. Veronica felt her shoulders tighten up as they continued near the red and yellow flowers.

She stopped, refusing to go any further.

Simper turned to her and smirked. "What is the matter?"

She returned his smile with a cold one of her own. "You really think I'm going to come any closer to those flowers, Simper? I don't know what you're trying to pull here, but I'm not going to fall for it."

He turned his head toward the flowers and shrugged. "My mistake. I didn't realize we were this close to them."

Veronica shook her head. "We can go around the garden from now on or stay away from it altogether."

He stood, staring at her for a moment. Then he smiled. "You need to learn self-control, Veronica. You need to learn to control your hormones, to control your sexual feelings. You need to focus your attention on the tasks at hand, not be consumed with thoughts of another. These are things you need to learn and learn quickly."

Veronica felt a warm tingling sensation across her skin again, like when she first encountered the Eros plant. She fought the feeling and pointed her finger at the man in front of her. "I'll learn those things in my own time, Simper. Without your help."

He shook his head. "Unfortunately, we don't have time for you to learn them on your own."

"What are you talking about?" The warm sensation was moving up into her thighs now. She felt her body trembling under the sensation. She felt warm all over, her chest beating rapidly with heat emanating off her blouse.

He pointed toward her feet. "You've been standing in a crop of newly planted Eros. Now is the time you will have to fight your urges."

She glared at him and then, when she tried to move, saw him thrust his hands out. She found herself unable to move more than a foot in any direction before an invisible wall impeded her.

"What do you think you're doing?!" She beat on the force field, feeling her strength rapidly depleting. The warming sensation moved between her legs and she suddenly fell to the ground, rubbing her hands along the inner parts of her thighs, trying to get the sensation to disappear like a bad itch.

Simper moved closer to her, just shy of the force shield he had put up. "Fight it, Veronica. Don't give in to your lusty desires. Don't give control of your body to a mere plant."

She found herself enthralled by this erotic feeling. Her hands made their way toward her crotch, but she quickly pulled them away as she closed her eyes to focus on getting out of this mess. Her chest was pulsing with pleasure now, echoing the rhythm she felt in between her legs.

Simper knelt and picked one of the small flowers that were in the ground near the outside of the barrier. Twirling it in his fingers, his beady eyes looked at her with confidence. "Fight it. I have overcome the desires associated with the body's natural reactions to sexual feelings. I have mastered it with my own iron will. You must if you want to continue along this path to perfection with me."

Veronica felt a flow of erotic images pass through her mind and she tried to stop each of them. Thoughts of sex and lust danced through her consciousness and only made the sensation that much stronger. She dropped to her knees. She felt she might begin moaning, but resisted the urge, keeping her mouth closed...her eyes closed. She moved her hands to her sides and allowed the sensation to continue between her legs.

She realized, with sudden horror, that she would not be able to contain this urge. The thoughts, the feelings, coursing through her were too strong. Pleasure pulsed through every part of her, and she knew the only escape was through, to give in to the urges, to accept her carnal nature.

But then, beyond hope, a voice entered her mind. It was peace. It was calm.

I will provide the way of escape.

Veronica did not recognize the voice. It had no tone, just spoke to her spirit in a very authoritative but calm manner.

She closed her eyes and took a deep breath. She breathed in the scent of cherry blossoms. She nodded. She wanted escape. She didn't want to succumb to these animalistic urges that Simper's plants caused.

But whose voice spoke to her? And what did they mean about a way of escape? She indeed wanted escape from this. She didn't want to cave in to her body's wants.

She tried to summon the voice, but it would not come at

her beck and call.

She felt her sexual urges suddenly subside. The pleasuring sensations left her body almost immediately, and she was left with clarity. Peace of mind. Calm of spirit.

Veronica took a few more deep breaths, exhaling slowly as she cleared her mind.

Then she opened her eyes and found Simper staring down at her from the other side of the shield, his gaze drinking in the cleavage of her blouse.

She wanted to kill him, yet, she had much more she had to pull from him. Much more she had to learn from him, all which she would use to upend him and whatever he had going on in secret.

She swallowed hard and drank in the truth that this had been more than a training exercise, more than a dirty trick. What if he had planned on raping her? To take advantage of her weakened sexual daze to go to town on her? She shook the disgusting thoughts from her mind and slowly stood to her feet.

His gaze returned to hers, and he smiled in a way that sent chills across her body. "You must learn to control yourself, first and foremost. If you cannot control yourself, then you cannot control the power of the Ancient Ones. If you cannot control yourself, you cannot control your fate. If you cannot control yourself, you cannot control the future. The truth of these things is the beginning of understanding."

She held her arms at her side and breathed, restraining every urge to kill him.

He lifted the flower to his nose, took a deep whiff, and then tossed it to the ground. He raised his hands and removed the shield.

She made no sudden movements, even though she wanted to slaughter him here and now. She had to play this game to its end. There could very well be more lives at stake than her own.

"You are an incredible being," he said, his eyes scanning her body as she stood. "You truly are the one worthy of harnessing the power of the Ancient Ones." He waved her away as he turned and started toward the house. "That is enough for today. Tomorrow, we will teach you to harness the power of the Ancient Ones. Go home and rest, for tomorrow will be your day of victory."

Veronica wanted to argue with him, give herself another excuse to search the house, but decided against it. Instead, she turned and headed home.

***

Sean was at the house when Veronica arrived home. He was drinking a glass of milk in the kitchen and his eyes seemed angered when she walked into the kitchen to grab a glass of water.

"Where have you been?" he asked.

She pulled a tall glass out of the cupboard and drew water from the filtered faucet on the kitchen sink. "None of your business."

Sean laughed, slamming the glass of milk down on the marble island as he drank the last of the white liquid. "You really think you're going to get away with that excuse?"

Veronica sipped some of her water, still recuperating from the effects of the Eros plant. "What do you mean get away? You're not dad or mom. What I do is really none of your business."

He nodded. "Okay, sis. If you don't want to talk to your brother, fine."

Here we go with the guilt trip. "Nice try. How about where have *you* been? I haven't seen you around. You out with your girlfriend or one of the thousand other ladies you've been seeing?"

He smiled. "So mature, sis. So mature."

He walked away and headed to his room. Veronica finished

her water while she stared out the kitchen window at the back-yard. She daydreamed about killing Simper. She could strangle him. Maybe stab him in that ugly face of his. She shook the thoughts from her mind, surprised at how morbid her feelings had suddenly become. Why did she suddenly have these strange thoughts and desires of killing that man?

Because he had tried to...well...

Veronica wanted to say he had tried to rape her. But he hadn't. He didn't lay a finger on her, even when she was almost writhing on the ground in a pleasurable state of mind. If he had made a move on her, while she had been in that position, would she have gone with it? Would she have had sex with him? She shuddered at the thought. Being that out of control scared her to her core. She couldn't allow that to happen again, no matter how badly she wanted to get to the bottom of the mystery surrounding him.

Veronica was proud of her virginity and didn't want to give it away to anyone...not her friends, not boyfriends, only to a husband. She didn't know why she felt so strongly about that, but she did. It was something built into her intricate core—no sex until marriage. She had seen too many people give their bodies away to complete strangers for no apparent reason. It wasn't going to happen to her though. She would save herself for the one who was meant for her...if he was even still out there.

The realization hit her hard: the skill and self-control that Simper had just taught her was invaluable, especially to her. How could she be mad at him for teaching her how to control her body and its sexual desires? He didn't touch her. He isolated her so she could learn the lesson on her own. In some ways, she felt gratitude in her heart for his extreme and unconventional actions.

On second thought though, Veronica realized it hadn't been Simper to actually teach her self-control. She had come so close to losing control. And then that voice, that whisper to her spirit, had calmed her body, turned off her uncontrollable urges.

Who or what had that been?

Veronica finished the water and set her glass down in the sink. Then she headed to her bedroom, changed into her pajamas, and then fell onto her bed. She felt a little better…a little safer…knowing she had overcome the effects of the Eros plant.

She slipped underneath her chilly covers and melted into the warmth of her bed as she slept peacefully that night.

CHAPTER 6

A Place to Herself

The next day, Veronica went to Simper's home. This time, he took her straight through the garden. The Eros plant indeed affected her, but she realized she slightly enjoyed the effect. The sensation, when exhibiting self-control, was nothing more than a slight tingling sensation across her arms and legs. The plant was clearly an aphrodisiac, one she had to take seriously but also learn more about.

Before heading to Simper's house that morning, Veronica researched the Eros plant online, but found nothing at all about the strange shrub. Had it been something Simper himself, or maybe Gloria Devine, had cultivated on their own?

They made their way toward the meditation room at the end of the garden, but Simper stopped them shortly before they reached the door.

"I am going to allow you to call forth the power for yourself. You have learned self-control. You have learned how to handle the energy from the gods. Now, I will teach you how to pull it out of the air yourself."

He led her into the small velvet room and motioned for her

to kneel. She positioned her knees on one of the soft pillows while Simper lit sticks of incense.

"Call on the Ancient Ones," Simper said, "and harness the power of the gods."

Veronica watched as he left the room, shutting the door behind him. She heard him engage a lock she didn't know the door had and had to fight the panic that almost immediately flooded her system. She had to remain calm, had to see this play out. She felt closer than ever to revealing what was behind Simper's 'curtain,' and she would do (almost) whatever it took to get to the end of this trail.

She took a deep breath. She was alone. Alone, with the smoky streams of vanilla and patchouli scent wafting through the air. She felt so relaxed. Being alone in this room settled her nerves and gave her some degree of peace. Of course, she didn't believe Simper's nonsense about the Ancient Ones. It seemed he was just able to pull energy—some type of energy—out of the atmosphere.

She wondered if she could do the same.

She closed her eyes, feeling the soft velvet on her bare knees. Wearing another skirt today was probably a bad idea, but she wanted to test her self-control and see if she could further seduce Simper to the point of revealing his true intentions with her. She believed he did want to train her, but for what purpose? He couldn't be all that concerned with helping her and her friends fight crime in Lysallis. No, he had other motives, another agenda, and she couldn't rest until she figured out what that was.

She readjusted herself, slipping her sneakers off so her feet could breathe. She knelt on the pillow again and closed her eyes, taking in a deep breath of the incense. She began by imagining the air in front of her. If Simper had just pulled stuff out of the air, and if she could do the same, then it should only be a matter of focusing on that air and imagining the particles that she

76

wanted her body to absorb from it.

She felt everything slow. She could suddenly hear the movement of Simper outside the doorway. He was nervous, anxious, eager to see her succeed in the task he set before her.

She could feel the cool air from outside, February's chill. She could sense the warmth of the ember on the end of the incense sticks.

She heard the mewling sound again, just outside her circle of focus. Instead of reaching toward that sound, instead of trying to grasp it, she instead just listened. She allowed her hearing to still, and in the surrender, she realized with some degree of horror that the mewling sounds were indeed cries.

Multiple people were crying. Sobbing. Whining.

Veronica pushed the realization to the side and focused on the room, specifically the air in the room.

She could see them now, the chemicals. They were purple in color. They were like dust particles existing side-by-side with the other elements in the air, such as oxygen and nitrogen and argon. She inhaled, and the purple particles began to move toward her, attracted to her like metal shavings to a magnet.

When the purple particles touched her skin, she felt her body absorb them. Her bones, her muscles, tingled with strange energy. It felt kind of good at first, but as she pulled in more and more of them, she felt pain. The energy started to burn inside of her. She fell to the ground, crying out in agony as it felt as if her whole body was suddenly on fire.

She heard the door open and Simper step in…then everything went black.

***

When Veronica opened her eyes, she found herself in a dark

room.

Her body was weak under the soft covers draped over her body. Her eyes adjusted to the darkness, and she slowly lifted these covers to find she was still clothed in the skirt and blouse she had on earlier, before blacking out. She was relieved to know she wasn't naked with Simper on top of her.

The thought made her gag.

She caught her breath and turned over to find the other half of the bed empty. This settled her nerves. It seemed she was alone.

She sat up, her head pounding in protest at the simple movement. She managed to find a switch for the light next to her bed. When she hit it, soft light flooded the room. She then noticed the tray of food on the nightstand. Bagels, juice, some fruit. She hesitated only for a moment, wondering briefly if Simper would poison her. She dismissed this possibility with the simple fact that he could have killed her when she blacked out. In fact, she realized with some embarrassment, he could have killed her a dozen times by this point.

The realization of her own carelessness weighed heavily on her. There was no real excuse.

She put her own self-scolding to the side and grabbed some strawberries and began nibbling on the fruit.

She realized she felt somewhat empty, as if that strange energy had burned everything out of her muscles and joints.

She heard a knock at the door. She pulled the covers up over herself. "Come in."

Simper entered the room, a huge smile on his face. "I am so happy you are alright."

She nodded, swallowing the strawberries she was eating. "Thank you for the food."

He nodded as he drew to her bedside. "Your body needs to

heal after what happened. You absorbed too much of the Ancient One's power and didn't release it before your body went haywire with it. You need to remember to release it. Form it into a globe of energy, like how I showed you."

She nodded.

"Listen, I am going to leave for a day. I have to head out of town. I was wondering if you would like to stay here and watch my home. This will give you a chance to get better and heal."

She sat up, almost unable to hide her excitement. "I would like that."

He smiled wider. "I know you are curious about me, Veronica. The whole house is open for you to investigate in the hopes you will learn to trust me completely. Not once since you've been here have I taken advantage of you. I haven't touched you or tried to make any romantic moves on you. You *can* trust me. But, so there is no doubt left in your mind, you may explore this place to the very best of your ability. Just please, do not pass across the black door. That is the sanctuary of the Ancient Ones."

"Sanctuary?" *Black door?*

He nodded and then started toward the door. "I will be back the day after tomorrow. Get your rest today and you can explore all day tomorrow if you want. Just don't disturb that one room, understand?"

She nodded. The very fact that he was telling her not to try that door was going to prompt her even moreso to do it.

But what if that was what he wanted? If you tell someone not to push the big red button, you have to know they are going to push it at the first opportunity. Was he using some kind of reverse psychology on her?

He wouldn't have to know.

After Simper left, Veronica ate more fruit and then relaxed in the bed, her thoughts wandering to the freedom she would have in exploring this place. She would have to craft a cleverer excuse to her friends and Sean as to where she was. Maybe an overnight stay somewhere relaxing to clear her mind? Would they believe that?

It wouldn't take more than a night to explore this place. She couldn't let it take more than a night. She didn't have that time, nor did she have the excuses to cover that time.

The deception she was having to weave between her friends and family disheartened her.

She placed her head back on the pillow and stared at the dark ceiling, shadows and light cutting a geometric pattern across its surface.

She fell asleep, dreaming of her adventures with the Lazerblades. They were fighting Mr. Big as usual, but this time, Big had a gun and shot David in the head. He died. Veronica cried in the dream, her chest heaving and convulsing at the thought of losing him.

She awoke in a sweat, scared at first when she didn't recognize the room. Then she calmed, reminding herself she was still at Simper's.

She turned to the clock and realized it was morning. *How long have I been asleep?*

She slid out of the bed and opened the curtains of the bedroom window. She hadn't known until now that she was on the second floor, looking over the garden area. It was beautiful from this view, with the different roses and tulips and ivy. She could make out the red and yellow colors of the Eros flowers as well, happy that she had overcome its debilitating effects.

She looked down at her skirt and blouse, realizing she didn't have a change of clothes. *Oh well.* She planned on spending most of the day exploring anyway. But first, she wanted to practice drawing power from the atmosphere. She slid her sneakers on (Simper had set them neatly on the floor beside her bed), and then made her way downstairs and out to the garden. She strolled through the plants without a second thought to the Eros flowers there, almost mocking her, trying to find some way of breaking through her mental block on their effects and strangle her in erotic thoughts and feelings.

She made her way to the velvet room. She lit some incense and knelt on the cushion, happy to have a whole day to herself. She closed her eyes and breathed in the vanilla and patchouli scents. She managed to concentrate hard enough, to allow herself to relax, to where she could feel the cool morning air from outside, sense the warmth from the incense stick, and hear moaning…moaning? She concentrated harder. The sound was painful moaning…and it sounded female. Was this the mewling she had been hearing? It seemed so loud and clear this time, not distant or out of reach.

Her concentration broke and her eyes opened. She could no longer hear it. She felt her pulse race. Where had that sound come from? She shook her head, realizing it could have been from anywhere, possibly even the surrounding neighborhood. It could have been her imagination.

She closed her eyes and focused again. This time, she overlooked the moaning and sought out the particles in the atmosphere. She could see them in her mind's eye, the purple particles of rhodenine. She drew them toward herself, slowly, carefully. She felt them enter her muscles and her bones.

She opened her eyes and held out her right palm. Concentrating, she watched as a dark orb began to materialize, dark-colored particles flitting through the air toward it, like moths to

81

an open flame.

Looking down at the sphere, she realized it was a violet in color, not black like Simper's. It was shining with such an incredible light...

She carried the globe outside toward the garden and thrust it out at one of the Eros plants, disintegrating it on contact. She smiled, giddy that she had finally learned how to do that. Her training was over with. She could use this power and protect David. Nobody had to know she even had it because it was a weapon that she could pull from anywhere within Anaisha. This would work well to put her mind at ease about David, and even in regard to protecting herself from people like Simper Creed.

She felt somewhat weak. It made sense that the process of drawing from Anaisha's atmosphere would weaken a person. It took incredible levels of focus and concentration. She stood in the garden, allowing her mind to rest, while she pondered her dream from the night before. Her feelings for David were strong, she realized. Too strong to be a simple friendship. Did she have *romantic* feelings for him? She couldn't...not when Carrie was her best friend and David was gaga in love with Carrie. Veronica's heart wrestled with frustration. She would never be able to ask David out because of his feelings toward Carrie and Carrie's feelings toward him, but they were never going to tell each other how they felt, so nobody was ever going to be with anybody.

Ridiculous!

Veronica shook the thoughts from her mind. She had learned how to harness the energy. Now was the time to explore. She wondered again where the painful moaning from earlier had come from. Was someone suffering somewhere on the property? She didn't want to think so, but she couldn't be sure unless she explored.

She figured she would start with the inside of his manor. The place was huge, and she wanted so badly to check out the black door. She would eventually. In case this was a test, in case he was actually watching her from afar, she would have to explore everything else first. If Simper was going to quell her training, she would rather it be after she had checked out every other square inch of this place.

Veronica started back across the garden and made her way into the house. She began by searching the kitchen area and the living room. Both areas turned up nothing but Simper's strange eating habits. In the fridge, she found strange stacks of white vegetables she couldn't identify. She pulled one of them out and set it on the island counter of the kitchen and stared at it for a moment. It smelled of chocolate...kind of. But it was pure white, hard, and had a green stem attached to the top of its cylindrical body. She thought to take a bite, but decided against it, putting it back into the refrigerator instead.

She found two piles of meat stacked side-by-side in the freezer. All of it was bright pink and caked in blood. It was organized in such a way that Veronica wondered if it was used to feed something other than Simper. She shuddered at the thought and made her way into the living room. There was nothing interesting there. Just a large TV, some couches, and chairs. A coffee table acted as a platform to a variety of female statues, all of them dressed in scantily clad apparel. It could be argued that they were artistic, but Veronica easily dismissed that possibility. She figured even though Simper had left her alone that day she struggled with the Eros plant, he was still a pervert. She could just sense that about him. She was uneasy anytime he was around.

She made her way upstairs and began to investigate the different rooms that all branched off the hallway. Each one turned up almost nothing. Almost. Veronica found scraps of articles in a desk drawer, all of them referencing the old woman who lived in this house before Simper. She really loved archaeology and she had spent most of her life savings on finding ancient artifacts that she believed to be weapons of some sort. Otherworldly weapons. Veronica was intrigued by these items but could find no other references to them in any other part of the house that she searched.

By the afternoon, she had searched almost the whole house, except for the room with the black door. She realized she would still have to wait to check that out. First, she would have to get some lunch and then check out the first room in the garden Simper had taken her to, the one with the newspaper articles. She felt there might be more to that room than what she could see or what Simper had shown her.

Eating in the manor wasn't going to happen, so Veronica left the property and headed to the local Bravo's Burgers. There, she purchased a combo meal number three: A double cheeseburger with extra meat, large fries, and a soda. She took a seat near a window in the fast food joint and ate by herself, pondering her own health and the situation she was in.

Her body felt lacking in nutrients, as if she hadn't eaten real food in days. She knew it had to do with the rhodenine that had burned its way through her muscle and bone. She had to be careful. Now she knew she couldn't use that energy too much or it would ruin her body, especially if she waited too long to release it. She imagined the rhodenine as some corrosive element that would eat away at her body if given the chance.

Sitting in the restaurant, Veronica let herself relax. The place wasn't very busy, and she enjoyed the space from Simper's place of residence. Something about that place felt like worms crawling underneath her skin. It wasn't until she was away from there that she realized how oppressive the environment really was.

She wanted out of this relationship with Simper. She would have to turn away from whatever else he wanted to teach her. She knew enough now, and it was time to move on with her life. She wanted to be back with her friends.

Regarding her found feelings for David, she would have to move on and find herself someone else, or maybe nobody at all, to spend her romantic life with. Either way, she would have to bury her own feelings for David, just like she had strangled the strange powers the Eros plant had over her, she would have to do that with the feelings she had for David. Maybe that strange force or presence that had quenched her erotic passions could help her quelch her feelings for David. She had to at least keep them under control, keep them out of David's sight and Carrie's sight. And especially out of the sight of her brother. If Sean found out that Veronica truly, madly loved David, then everything would blow up in her face.

Veronica finished her sandwich and started on her fries, wondering what David and Carrie were doing at this moment in time. Were they together? Were they all wondering where she was at? Veronica looked up in time to see David walk into the restaurant...alone! She shoved some fries in her mouth and chewed fast, realizing she would have to leave before—

He was already making his way toward her. She threw out curses in her mind. This was going to be awkward and tense.

David took a seat across from her, his green eyes sparkling out at her. She felt her heart skip a beat and realized she had to get herself under control. She took a sip of her soda and waved at him. "Hey, David."

He smiled at her but didn't say anything at first. He glanced around the room, probably making sure there wasn't any trouble nearby as he always did. His face had his usual 5 o'clock shadow, and his short brown hair looked unruly today.

He leaned in toward her and spoke. "Veronica, we're all a bit curious as to what you've been up to lately. You've been gone all night and now I find you here, in a Bravo's Burgers, scarfing down fries?"

She stared at him for a moment, trying to get over his beautiful eyes. She felt so tired and so emotional. She picked her words carefully, knowing they wouldn't do any good to deter David from being suspicious of what she was up to. He truly cared for her—and the rest of the team—and if he became too suspicious, he would rip open her life until he figured out what was going on.

"I…"

David held his hand up, giving her a fatherly glare. "I don't want excuses, V. I want you to tell me what's really going on. No lies."

Why would he think she would lie to him?

Because she would. Like right now.

She mustered up her courage and explained to him that she had just been fighting depression. With Mr. Big in the wind and the winter settling in, she was feeling down and just wanted some time to herself to figure some things out.

He stared at her for a few moments. She had an urge to lean out and kiss him. Why didn't she ever act on these feelings earlier, back when she had just met him? Because she fell in love with him these years since he had saved her life. He wasn't just Anaisha's greatest hero. He was her greatest hero.

He narrowed his eyes on her. "I don't completely believe you, but I'll let it go. Just promise me you'll tell me if there's something wrong. We're here for you. I'm here for you."

That last line. It made her heart flutter.

"How are you and Carrie doing?" she asked.

He shrugged. "I don't know. Good, I guess. We haven't done much over the last couple days. We saw Sean yesterday. He's getting on my nerves as always."

She nodded. "He is my brother. And he is annoying."

David grinned slyly. "Want me to join you for lunch or do you have somewhere to be?"

She felt herself blush. "I'd love that."

David got up and stood in line to order food. Veronica looked down at her watch. It was already two. If she hung out with David for a couple hours, then that would only leave a couple hours of daylight to search the rest of the mansion grounds. She decided she would have to risk it. If she had to, she could find some flood lamps or flashlights, or something.

David grabbed some food and sat across from her.

She had nowhere she would rather be.

CHAPTER 7

Underneath the Mask

Hours later, Veronica and David parted ways.

Reluctantly, on Veronica's part.

She couldn't remember very many moments like that in her time knowing David. Just a quiet lunch. Time with him, without everyone else around.

They ate, and they talked about random life things. He wanted to know how her fashion line was going. She shrugged at that and mumbled something about it being in the works. Truth was, she hadn't touched her fledgling fashion enterprise in a while, especially with all the nonsense with Simper. She missed designing dresses and skirts and accessories.

She asked him more than once about his status with Carrie. He shrugged the question away each time. She thought he would grow increasingly irritated being asked about it so often, but he didn't seem to show it. Each time, he shrugged and then looked off in the distance at something or someone.

The restroom had grown increasingly busy, but she had managed to drown out the background noise and give David her full attention. Maybe it was due to her newly learned skills, but she found it easier to focus, easier to narrow down the distractions to the ones she wanted to put her attention to.

Veronica returned to the mansion, but it was already five, meaning she would only have about an hour before the sun started to set. She figured the meditation room would have to be the final place she investigated today. She knew there wasn't anything too interesting in the garden (besides the Eros plants) and nothing really caught her attention on the rest of the grounds outside the house.

Veronica made her way through the garden, watching with a close eye at how close she came to the Eros plants. She had those intense feelings for David earlier and didn't want to take any risks that the Eros plant would increase those feelings. She wondered if her interactions with the plant in the last couple days could have led to her feelings for David.

Don't lie, she told herself. She knew for a fact that she had been feeling something for David for a while now, not just today. Today just seemed to be the…peak…of those feelings and emotions.

She stopped at the door to the meditation room and wondered for a moment if she was truly in love with David. Despite her vow not to make a move toward him while Carrie was still alive, she realized that she did have actual feelings for him. Not just surface feelings, but actual love for him. He was kind, courageous, handsome…he had his faults, she knew they all had their faults, but his were easily forgivable.

Veronica opened the door and peered inside the velvet room. It was dark. She flipped on a light switch and shut the door behind her. She wasn't sure who else would have access to Simper's mansion and so she didn't trust herself being out here too late by herself.

If only she could have told David about this place, about that evil man, then he could have come out here with her to help destroy him. But instead, she was alone. Because of her secrets, she was by herself, snooping around a dangerous man's property for something she probably didn't really want to find.

She left the meditation room and ventured into the small shed. The newspaper articles posted to the walls were a bore to her now, just the strange infatuations of a man gone mad, believing there were such beings known as gods who gave him these strange powers he was so intent on teaching her about. Veronica found nothing more than gardening equipment.

She realized the sun was going to be setting soon, and she really didn't want to be here another night alone. She would have to finish up her search soon and then head home to the safety of her warm and comforting bed.

Veronica started back across the garden area, once again being mindful of the Eros plants. When she reached the house, she realized the only choice she had now was to enter the room with the black door. She would have to run in, check things out, and escape the house before Simper came back. She knew he would find out if she went through that door, and the knowledge of this sent chills down her spine. But to not go through it, to ignore it, would be ignoring some bigger issue. Simper had secrets. Dark secrets. Veronica knew nothing of the source of his power, but she figured its root had to be found in something pretty debasing. If she didn't stop him, if she didn't uncover whatever was going on here, she could be responsible for whatever happened next.

She walked up the stairs, realizing she could possibly check his room as well. She hadn't been in there yet. *Maybe that's where I should start.* She turned and went back down the stairs and found his room on the first floor near the base of the stairs. His door was shut. Before entering, Veronica made sure to check for any traps he may have set, like little pieces of tape or markers to indicate when someone had opened the door. She didn't find any, and so she turned the knob and walked into the dark room.

Black curtains covered his window, blocking any chance of the sunset coming into the house. The darkness seemed to hinder her breathing. It was thick, and there was a strange smell she couldn't seem to pinpoint...something like vanilla, but blended with something else that smelled rotten, like expired meat.

She stumbled along the wall and found the light switch, revealing Simper's room to be quite basic.

Everything in the room was black. The bed sheets, the bedposts, the desk, the walls. Even the floors were covered in thick black carpet. A small black desk sat in the corner beside a large four-post canopy bed.

She made her way to the desk, searching the immaculately clean surface for anything that may reveal more of what Simper was involved in. But she found nothing. She sat on the bed and buried her head in her palms, thinking of how ridiculous it was that she was even here, that she was even probing through someone else's things. It was a ridiculous idea. She realized she wanted to go home. Forget the black door, forget everything she was paranoid about. She learned a new skill, a new defense to protect David. Now it was time to quit while she was ahead.

It was time to go home. It was time to leave this behind her.

A voice, small and still, crept into her ears, slid into her spirit. *Help them.*

She didn't hear the voice really, more she felt it in her spirit. Calm. Soothing. Authoritative. Just like before, when it calmed her during the effects of the Eros plant.

"Help who?" she whispered.

Then she heard the mewling. The cries of of the women she

91

heard in days past. The sound of their whines was faint at first, but the more Veronica focused on them, the louder they became.

They were in agony, crying out for death, for reprieve from their torture.

Veronica scrambled around the room to find a trap door of some sort. The voices were coming from underground, but she couldn't pinpoint exactly where.

She checked under the bed and pulled at different points of the carpet to expose an entryway of any sort. She checked the closet and found a row of hangers, all holding cloaks in shades of midnight and void. She rustled through Simper's wardrobe, her hands brushing across the back wall in hopes of finding a secret switch of some sort.

But she found nothing.

The voices were in full clarity now, angst filling their whines and cries. Multiple women in tortured pain, but Veronica couldn't figure out how to reach them.

Then that still small voice came through again: *The garden.*

She turned and looked out the bedroom window at the garden outside. Dusk spilled across the various plants, and it suddenly made perfect sense to her that that's where he would hide a lair if he had one.

Veronica dashed out to the garden, her heart racing. Once in the midst of the plants, she frantically searched the ground for a trap door or latch of some kind.

It dawned on her that she was standing in the middle of recently-planted Eros plants, the small leaves of which brushed against her bare legs. She felt warmth pour across her skin and travel up into her thighs. The tingling became unbearable, and she stumbled out of the plants and hit the ground on her rear end.

She felt an overwhelming sensation of lust take over. She

fought it, pulling the endangered women to the forefront of her mind in an attempt to override the hostile ambush from the Eros plant.

"No," Veronica whispered as she felt the sensation move through her arms, her shoulders, her neck.

Every inch of her body felt pleasurable. She looked down and realized she was sitting directly in the center of the patch of Eros plants, the leaves aggressively caressing every part of her exposed skin.

Her mind buzzed and she shook her head, trying to toss the feeling. "The girls. I have to help them," she whispered.

I will help you.

The voice again. Who was speaking to her? Into her? There was nothing sensual about the voice. It was commanding, direct, confident. Full of power.

Suddenly, in a split second, the feelings of lust and sexual desires fled her body.

Veronica sat in the patch of Eros plants, her body completely unaffected by the plant's erotic nature.

Her hands found purchase in the soil. She went to push herself up to her feet when her right hand felt something metal. A ring. She looked down and realized it was the handle to a trap door she had been sitting on.

Veronica scrambled to her feet. She brushed the soil from her legs and her skirt, then she reached down and pulled on the ring, opening a square wooden door. She peered down the shaft. A ladder ran down into a dark abyss.

Veronica retrieved a flashlight and a small knife from the kitchen, cursing herself for not bringing the pocketknife she had on her the other day. She had been so preoccupied with everything that she had even managed to neglect arming herself (however well a pocketknife could possibly protect her).

She thought to rush home and get better supplies, but Simper could come back at any time, so this may be her only chance to save the women who were in trouble.

She glanced behind her at the setting sun. It was now hidden below the horizon, out past the outline of the dark house. Night had arrived. The air was growing chilly now that the garden was being consumed by darkness.

Shining the light down into the shaft, the beam refused to reach the bottom. All she could make out was a rusty iron ladder that vanished into darkness a few feet down. Against her better judgement, Veronica tucked the knife in the back of her skirt, then mounted the ladder with flashlight in hand. She climbed down a couple feet and then reached up and pulled the trapdoor shut.

She knew there was a chance she could get locked down here.

She knew she should have contacted her friends.

She knew the police should have known about this place by this point in time.

She knew a lot of things.

She also knew these women—whoever they were—were counting on her to save them.

She started down the ladder. A chilly breeze shot up the shaft, running its cold fingers up her skirt. Her thighs froze at the contact of the wind, and she felt the chill through her whole body.

A variety of smells hit her, but none of them were unfamiliar to her. It smelled of sewage. Of body odor. Of death and rot.

She was descending into darkness, both figuratively and literally. Her spirit grew heavy as she made her way deeper underground, and she had to fight the urge to climb back up the ladder and get as far away from Simper's home as possible.

There were girls down here, girls who were in danger, in

torture, and they needed her to help them.

Veronica found herself glancing up the ladder every now and then to see if the trapdoor had been opened, to see if Simper had decided to pursue her.

But nothing was up there. Nobody was coming.

She traveled down the ladder for a minute and then shined the light down to found stained cement looking back up at her. Her feet found purchase on the floor, and she shined the light to find herself at the starting point of a narrow cement corridor. When she shined the light down the corridor, she saw cobwebs hanging from the arched ceiling. They moved with a breeze that rushed through the passageway, bringing with it damp air that smelled of rotting things. Something—or somethings—had definitely died down here at some point.

Veronica leaned against the wall for a moment to stop herself from retching. She pulled at the bottom of her skirt, trying her hardest to cover as much of her bare flesh as possible. She felt exposed, naked almost. There was an incredible sense of foreboding filling up her spirit. Something wrong was down here. Something dark. Evil.

She collected herself and then started down the corridor, lighting the path well enough so that nothing would have the opportunity to jump out at her. There were no doors along the corridor, just dark-stained cement that curved into a ceiling. There was enough room in the passageway for her to reach her arms out to her sides and touch the walls with her fingertips. The walls themselves had mildew and mold growing on them. Veronica lifted her blouse up over her nose and mouth to keep from breathing in the fumes.

She moved down the corridor, her thoughts racing. What if Simper found her down here? Would he attempt to kill her?

Common sense caught up with her, and she realized she was doing a very stupid thing coming down here by herself without at least alerting David or Carrie to what she was up to. Had she really grown this stubborn that she couldn't expect her friends to help her when she was in trouble?

And she was in trouble. Rummaging through a madman's mansion, someone who possessed the power to vaporize her if he so chose. She suddenly realized that if he did choose to vaporize her, there would be no evidence, no indication that she was ever here. How long would it take for one of her friends to realize she was actually missing? Would their investigations lead to Simper's place? What if he vaporized them too?

Veronica stopped and took a deep breath calming the panicked thoughts spiraling through her mind.

She continued down the long, mold-ridden corridor.

Up ahead, her light revealed a large opening. She turned the flashlight off and held the knife tight in her hand as she peered ahead, her feet stepping softer across the grimy cement. She could see nothing but patches of darkness and flickering candlelight dancing like ghosts in this dark place.

When she reached the end of the hallway, she peered into the opening and discovered a large chamber. It had to be at least four times the size of the gym at her old high school, the ceiling rising so high she couldn't see the top of it. Sconces embraced the walls, lighting up fragments of the dungeon, revealing iron cages set on the floor, most filled with people.

Veronica stood, staring in awe at the horrific scene before her, ignoring the cries of the prisoners once they saw her enter the room. Her stomach twisted in knots, and she dropped to her knees, her kneecaps feeling the slippery grime of the dungeon floor.

Arms extended from a cage to her right. A female voice, hoarse and ragged, cried out to her. "Help us, stranger! Please." The woman's voice trailed off at the end, and if Veronica hadn't turn to see the minute spark of life in the woman's eyes, she would have sworn she had died at the end of her sentence.

As she took in the room, Veronica saw that almost every cage had a female occupant. Most of them were young, bedraggled with their clothes torn or missing, and their hair disheveled and caked in dirt and grime. The girls seemed weak, their eyes void of anything eliciting life. Their forms were clearly malnourished by the way their bony figures shifted within their cages, arms and legs mimicking those of marionettes.

"What is going on?" Veronica mumbled, though she had a partial idea of what was occurring here. Simper had kidnapped these girls and used them.

But for what purpose?

The insinuations filling Veronica's mind threatened to send her into a fit. Had he used all these girls for sex? Had he raped each one of these prisoners? How long had most of them been here?

Veronica's heart dropped when she realized she had been able to hear their voices days ago. She could have rescued them days ago.

She could have killed Simper Creed days ago.

The woman in a cage to her left stirred, shifting her anemic form so she could extend frail arms through the bars toward Veronica. "Please. Please get me out of here."

Veronica knelt, setting her flashlight and on the floor before taking the woman's hands into her own. Her skin felt like dried leather, and her cage smelled of urine. The woman looked up at Veronica through a veil of scraggly brown hair. Veronica could tell by the dancing firelight that the woman's eyes were blue, however, one of them was pale, indicating she was blind in that eye. The other eye showed the remnants of a color that may once have sparkled like a dazzling sapphire. Her clothes hung off her body like dime store hand-me-downs. Her black skirt was torn, her blue blouse was faded. She was barefoot, and her arms carried dozens of scars across her skin.

"My family needs me," she whispered, her voice scratchy. "My husband. My childr—" She yanked her arms back into the cage and embraced herself, sobbing.

Veronica stared at the woman. The other girls in the room pleaded for help, their voices rising, the room filling with a cacophony of tortured souls.

"What's your name?" Veronica asked the woman.

The woman stared at her.

Veronica lunged at the bars, wanting to break them in half with her bare hands. But the metal was thick. A giant lock hung from the cage door. Veronica could pick it if she had the right tools.

"Luena."

Veronica acknowledged the name. "Luena. I'm going to get you out of here, Luena."

A slight grin crept across Luena's face. Her mouth opened slightly, and Veronica caught sight of her teeth. The front two were chipped. The woman's mouth opened wide, and she laughed. Veronica saw a strange symbol on the woman's wrist—a blue plus sign with a dot in each of its four corners.

Luena followed Veronica's gaze, then she turned her wrist in shame. "He branded us."

The other occupants of the dungeon started to wail. Fear struck Veronica. She stood to her feet and turned to find Simper standing feet from her, staring at her with those beady black eyes. He was calm and seemed unaffected by her intrusion into his little dungeon.

"Welcome, Veronica. I knew if I left you to your own devices, you would eventually find it."

She was speechless. He actually wanted her to find this horrid place?

"You look surprised."

She grimaced. "What is this? What do you think you're doing here?"

He stretched his arms out toward his captives. "These are the very sources of my income, dear Veronica."

"What?"

"They are my bargaining chips in this darkened world. Some of them I sell through slavery on the black market. Some of them are sacrificed to the Ancient Ones."

"Sacrificed? Are you crazy?!" Veronica reached to the back waistline of her skirt and felt for the knife handle there.

Simper's eyes glimmered. "I get the feeling that crazy question wasn't rhetorical. Listen to me and I will tell you a story." He motioned for her to follow him as he snaked his way through the maze of cages, the candlelight flickering across his black cloak like flames in a burning building. She reluctantly went with him, everything within her suppressing her desire to kill him here and now.

"See, I took this house from the old woman you were researching earlier this week. She died because I needed to get my hands on what she was studying—ancient weapons that could potentially destroy those of the spiritual realm. She found a few sets of these weapons and hid them on this property. I killed her, took the house, and found some of these weapons. There are others out there, others that I need. In order to get them, I need money, and to get that money, I sell these sad looking pawns on the black market."

"Sell them?"

He nodded. "Into slavery. Sometimes for work, most of the time for sex. Sometimes their bodies…" He stopped, glaring at one of the younger-looking girls who had retreated into the corner of her cage. "Sometimes their bodies are used for things…experiments and the likes. I don't necessarily agree with what I do, especially since they could be used as sacrifices, but I have to make money."

Veronica realized she was clenching her fists so heard her fingernails pierced her palms. "You're insane!!"

He shrugged. "I have to sacrifice them to the Ancient Ones. In return, the gods grant me their power. How do you think you obtained your power? I sacrificed a child in your name, Veronica. Her name was Lily." Simper studied Veronica, his eyes searching her face for some kind of reaction to what he said.

Veronica put on her best poker face, but it didn't really matter. She knew Simper knew how she felt about all of this.

All of this had been a trap.

"Lily cried before I took her from this world and passed her to the world beyond."

Dizziness hit Veronica. She leaned against the nearest cage to balance herself. Her head swam with the reality of the situation. She thought Simper was crazy. Mad. Insane.

Instead, she realized he was evil.

I have to pull David and Carrie into this. I have to call the police. I need to get help.

"I'm not going to stop you from calling the authorities, Veronica. I understand you don't agree with what I am doing here, but you don't really have a say in it. You are trespassing on my property. These girls are my property, and you can't have them. Nobody can have them unless they are willing to pay the price.

Also understand that if you try to come back here with your friends, they will find out about your exploits here. They will find out about your secrets, and I will end up killing them with the powers the Ancient Ones have bestowed upon me."

"No." She shook her head, realizing that this was more important than her secrets. David had to know. He had to help her stop this madman.

"Yes. I will kill your friend, David. And if you don't watch yourself, I will make *you* my slave as well."

Veronica's heart dropped into her stomach at the thought. She found herself breathing heavily, her blood coursing through her body at a frantic rate at thoughts of his evil schemes. She narrowed her eyes and clenched her fists. "I'm going to kill you." She reached for the knife at her back but found nothing there. Had she dropped it?

He smiled wickedly. "Yes. Kill me. I want you to. Once you kill me, I will join the Ancient Ones. You will finally fulfill your destiny."

"What are you talking about?"

"You are meant to kill me. That is the only way you can exceed the level your friends are at. They know nothing of how to kill…to destroy…to bring this world to its knees." His eyes glimmered with firelight. The prisoners all stared at Simper and Veronica, their eyes glazed, the spark of life nearly gone from each of them. "Complete your training and kill me. Allow me the privilege of spending tonight with the gods."

Veronica pushed past him and headed back through the room, toward the entrance to the grimy corridor. She knew she couldn't take him by herself. She would have to alert David and Carrie. Maybe even Sean. She withdrew her cell phone, but she had no signal this far down underground. She put the phone away and resolved that she would also need to involve the police. But what if some of them were on Simper's side? What if some of them had purchased these girls like cattle or product? The thought made her sick. Some of those girls looked about her age—around 18 or 19, just young women. But Luena was much older. And though she didn't want to admit it, Veronica thought some of the girls looked much younger, maybe in their teens. Maybe even younger...

She reached the ladder and climbed quickly.

The sun had set, and cold air moved through the garden, striking her like a serpent when she finally crawled up out of the hole in the ground.

He mentioned special weapons on the property. Would it be advantageous for her to find one of them and use it to destroy him?

If she involved her friends, if she called the police, Simper could very well kill all of them. She remembered watching him decimate that building in downtown Lysallis. What was to say he wouldn't do that to a squad of police or to her friends?

She ran toward the mansion. She ran as fast as she could, knowing all those girls were in grave and immediate danger, and she was the only one who could help them.

She burst into the building, rushed up the stairs, and stopped in front of the black door. The strange symbols carved around the frame were foreign to her. Were they telling her something in another language? Were they a warning?

She stepped back and lunged herself at the door. She heard a crack, but the door neither budged nor caved. She stepped back some more, a dull pain flashing through her shoulder now. She glanced down the hallway, expecting to see Simper coming to try and stop her.

She ran at the door headstrong and slammed her shoulder

into it again. She heard another crack, but she bounced off the door, stumbling backwards, her shoulder throbbing. There was a visible crack in the center of the blackened wood now though and this fueled her hope.

She took another step back and rubbed her shoulder. She could feel it bruising now. She took a deep breath and took another run at the door. She slammed into it as the wood cracked and the door splintered around her.

Veronica tumbled into darkness, falling into a black abyss void of any and everything.

She heard laughing. Wind blew around her, tossing her through the darkness. She tried to pull at her skirt, to tuck it down over her knees, but the wind was so violent, as if it was intentionally attacking her.

The laughing…it sounded muffled and deep. It scared her. She wished she had gotten David and Carrie to help her. She wished she could have said goodbye to David. To tell him how she felt about him…

She passed out, flailing through the darkness.

CHAPTER 8

Her Invisible Rescuer

When she opened her eyes, Veronica expected to find herself at home, in her bed. She expected to see the sun peering through the blinds of her bedroom window. She expected to feel the warmth of the heater blowing down on her while she lay comfy and cozy under her thick comforter.

Instead, she opened her eyes to darkness. At first, she panicked, thinking she may be blind. Then memories rushed in of her busting through the black door and hurtling into a darkness she had never known.

As she regained consciousness, she realized she wasn't falling anymore. She was standing on solid ground, but her arms were pinned to her side by an invisible force that was much stronger than her.

Someone—or something—laughed, and it sent terror through her bones.

She struggled against the invisible restraints, but to no avail.

"It is useless to try." The voice was deep and loud.

Her own body began glowing with a purple light. She suddenly felt something pulling the energy—the very life—out of her.

"If you cooperate, we will allow you to live."

"Who are you?" Her skin, her bones, her muscles were being tugged at. Violently. She felt teeth ripping at her arms, but when she turned her head, nothing was there, and her arms looked unscathed. But the pain was still there.

She groaned in agony.

"We are the Ancient Ones!"

The Ancient Ones? This couldn't really be happening. She wondered if this was some sort of trick by Simper.

A bright light suddenly blinded her. When the light paled, her eyes focused and she realized she was in an endless, white-tiled room. The floors, the ceiling, the walls were all made of dingy white tile, like the kind found in old locker room showers. She was in a room that went on to no distinguishable end. No doors, just walls. It filled her heart with terror.

What is this place?

Simper appeared from behind her, shaking his head as he stopped in front of her. "I had a feeling you would try to get into this space. I wished you to not come here, that is why I told you to stay away from the black door. But you refused to heed my objection. And now they require your blood."

She struggled against the invisible restraints but found her effort waning. She was indeed having power siphoned from her, but from who or what? "What are you talking about? Let me out of here!!"

"Screaming will do you no good." His lips thinned, his face aglow with purple light, and he seemed to smile, but not in a pleasant way. "We are in a place between time and space. You broke through the black door and entered the territory of the Ancient Ones. They aren't happy about that."

Her eyes felt heavy. The force holding her upright suddenly vanished, and she fell to the tile flooring hard, hitting her chin as bone cracked and her teeth clashed together.

"I did not want this for you, Veronica. I wanted peace. I wanted to teach you the ways of the Ancient Ones, the power of the Ancient Ones. But you did not want it. You wanted to pry. You wanted to investigate. I left for a day so you could get that out of your system. You found my dungeon and I still allowed you to live. Instead of being gracious about my mercy, you ran back here to do the unthinkable.

"I bet you were wondering what those symbols carved into the door were."

Veronica's voice wasn't strong enough to mutter any type of word. She tried to move on the floor, but her body just lay there haphazardly, her arms spread out, her knees buckled, her jaw throbbing. Fatigue gripped her.

"Those carvings in the door were protective carvings...of the three ancient chosen ones that will bring an end to this world. Those carvings contained the power of those chosen ones and were protecting our world from the domain of the Ancient Ones. When you breached that protective barrier, you ushered yourself into a place that doesn't even exist on our plane. This is nowhere, a nothingness in the middle of time and space and matter."

Veronica felt her lungs struggling to produce the oxygen needed to stay alive. It hurt to breathe in the stale air of this strange place. Was this really a place between space and time or was he bluffing? Were those voices she heard really the Ancient Ones or a giant hoax? She would never find the answers to her questions. This would be the end of things. She felt her eyes close and felt her spirit struggle with the very idea that Luena— and all those other girls and young women—would die at the hands of Simper.

At the hands of gods.

"The Ancient Ones have taken most of your life force. You will die in a short time. I have to say that I admired you." He bent down so he could whisper in her ear. "I'll make sure your friends in the dungeon get a humane death since you cared so much about them. I'll even tell David that you died trying to protect them...which isn't really that far from the truth, now is it?"

Veronica closed her eyes and felt the darkness sweeping over her.

So this is what death feels like? Her body, broken. Her spirit, drained. Her hope, shattered. Her friends, gone.

A still small voice within her nudged her to open her eyes, to lift herself off the floor. *Get up. You are not gone yet. This is not over.*

Her spirit screamed out David's name, as if he could hear her and would come to rescue her like the prince that he was.

But nothing came to save her.

Get up, the voice said again, gently, commanding.

She felt death's tendrils wrap around her, and she leaned into their embrace.

CHAPTER 9

Between Worlds

Veronica's eyes fluttered open. She lay on the floor of the unending tile room. The floor was cold against her cheek and her bare legs. She took a deep breath. Her lungs stung, but they delivered the oxygen her body craved.

She felt strength in her arms. She pushed herself off the floor and managed to sit up. The unending room was empty. No Simper. No strange god draining the life out of her.

No, it was just her.

And me.

The voice, still and soft in her spirit, was completely unknown to her. It was the same voice she heard when she repelled the effects of the Eros plant.

"Who are you?" she whispered. *"Please, tell me."*

The One True God.

Veronica shook her head. She knew of many gods. She knew of many fake gods.

She slowly stood to her feet, her knees nearly buckling at the motion.

The air was stale and lukewarm. It almost felt like nothing.

Neither hot nor cold, but Veronica realized that was impossible.

She glanced around the room and realized it went on forever in both directions, with walls framing it into something that resembled one large corridor.

No furniture.

No people.

Nothing but dingy tile.

She took a few more deep breaths, glad to get oxygen—and life—back into her body.

She heard a click, and suddenly a black door appeared to her left in the tiled wall.

When she approached, she saw that the frame had no symbols or etchings around it. The door was black in color, metallic almost, and the knob was bright silver.

She turned the knob and pushed the door open.

Another room stood on the other side. A small room, wood flooring, brown-painted walls, and display racks full of various weapons and their descriptions.

Are these the ancient weapons that Simper was speaking of? The ones Gloria Devine hunted down and collected?

Veronica stepped through the door. It vanished behind her in a mist, and all that remained was the brown-painted wall. The room was smaller than it looked from the other side of the black door. It seemed more like a shed than an actual room. An ordinary door stood to her right, shut. She wondered where it led. But before she would venture out that way, she was determined to arm herself.

Simper was going to die tonight. One way or another.

Veronica examined the weapons, one by one, hoping to find one that had the potential to kill Simper and whatever dark magic he had been operating in. Each weapon was on a display or in a glass case, and with them were little note cards with handwriting that described the individual weapons. She wondered if Simper or Gloria herself had written them out.

There was a sword on the wall, one that would supposedly call upon lightning.

A spear was affixed vertically to the wall, said to create magenta fire.

A dagger sat nestled in a velvet cloth within a glass case. The notecard told Veronica it was a poisonous blade that would inject an otherworldly substance into its victim that would then manifest weeks later in the form of a fatal disease. A note on the bottom of the card said that the blade had been named *Pestilence*.

A round wooden shield sat on the only table in the room. It wasn't in a display case, and it was surrounded by small rags and a flask of what looked to be gold-colored olive oil. Someone had clearly worked the surface of the wood recently as it had a shimmering shine to it. But there was nothing remarkable about the shield. It seemed to be made of old planks of wood. There were no metal brackets running around it or across it. Nothing adorned the shield.

A notecard sat propped up against the oil flask with only one word written on it: UNDETERMINED.

The final weapon in the room is what caught Veronica's eye. It was almost as if the items of interest drew her attention specifically, because Veronica found the sword, spear, dagger, and shield to be unremarkable when compared to the set of half-moon shaped blades that were displayed crisscross on the wall in a glass display case.

Veronica inspected the weapons, peering through the glass at the ornate design of the killing machines.

Each half-moon blade was about a foot long. Each had two handles attached—one apparently for spinning the blades around, and the other for holding the blades stationary in a blade-to-blade fight.

Two notecards were set into the case with the blades, a long string of description written out for the weapons. But these notecards were written out in handwriting different than the notecards included with the other weapons in the room.

This handwriting was messier, with the loops and lines more haphazard. The tone was different too—not someone simply describing some *thing*, but someone actually attesting to the history, the lore, the very life of the blades.

Scion Blades

These ancient blades come from the Fringe, a no-man's-land. They were found buried in volcanic rock at the site of Freesia Wood, a small village that operated at the base of the Heemoty Volcano. Various journals found within the ruins of Freesia Wood tell us these blades were worshipped for their powers. If one learned the dark arts associated with them, they could pull rhodenine from Anaisha's atmosphere and imbue it into the blades, temporarily, to give them powerful abilities.

My research has been ongoing in an attempt to find a way to permanently imbue the blades with the properties associated with rhodenine. Unfortunately, rhodenine is incredibly unstable and difficult to research or study to any safe or viable degree.

Many call rhodenine the power of the gods, but that is nonsense. It is an element within Anaisha's atmosphere, though one we still have so much to learn from.

Gloria Devine

Veronica's hands reached out to pull open the glass case.

111

She blinked, and the blade handles were in her palms.

Her eyes glittered with the awe she felt over these weapons.

She studied the blades. They were gorgeous. Black metal with an etched line of purple dye that ran the length of the blade. Veronica held them in her hands and began spinning them around on the handles that stuck out toward her. They spun as if they had just been oiled, the blades whirring at the sides of her face. She felt empowered, enabled, with these weapons. It felt good to spin them, to hold them. To have them. Somehow, she knew these were meant for her, made for her.

She narrowed her eyes. She had to get back to the dungeon and save those women before Simper could strip them of any more of their innocence.

She glanced around at the other weapons, realizing she would have to come back for them later. There didn't seem to be a harness for the blades she held, so she had no way of carrying all these weapons with her right now. The shield in particular interested her. Apparently, neither Gloria nor Simper had come to understand what qualities the defensive item had. What if it held a power that was world-changing?

Veronica shook her head. She would have to ponder these things later. Those girls needed her.

She opened the door on the other side of the little shack and found herself in the garden. When she stepped out of the doorway, the door slammed shut behind her. She turned and found there to be no shack. No room. Just a patch of Eros plants.

She returned to the trap door and took it back down to the grimy corridor.

This time, she didn't feel fear. Only anger and determination.

Simper had to die. There was no doubt about it in her mind

now. But would she be able to kill him? To destroy an uncommon evil such as himself?

Veronica raced down the corridor, a blade in each hand. The weapons felt natural in her grip. The weight of them seemed to balance her, tether her to this plane of existence.

When she reached the dungeon, she found most of the women had been taken from their cages. All the women but Luena, who Veronica found in the corner of her cage, her ratty hair covering her face as she pulled her knees to her chest, her body unmoving.

Veronica spun the blades in her hand and struck the bars of the iron chamber. The metal of the blades struck the bars with a loud clinking sound but did nothing to cut—or even damage—the iron.

Where had the girls gone in the small amount of time she had been in the other world?

Luena was alive. Veronica knew this because the bedraggled girl looked up at her, her one blind eye pleading for escape from this evil place.

"I want to help you," Veronica said.

The girl coughed. "I know."

"Where did he take the others?"

She buried her face in her knees for a moment. Then she looked up at Veronica. "To be sacrificed…because of what you did to the Ancient Ones."

"What *I* did?"

She nodded, looking thoughtful now. "You defiled their holy sanctuary. You intruded on their world and destroyed the barriers between both of our worlds. They are angry at the human race for what you just did."

All this talk of these invisible creatures was making Veronica's blood boil.

She looked down at the blades and realized these weapons

had come to her not by accident, but by intention. By purpose.

That still, small voice creeped into her mind, her spirit, again. *Save them.*

She closed her eyes and held the blades out in front of her. She took a deep breath, inhaling the musty stench of the dungeon: sweat, blood, tears. She could feel the fire from the sconces. She could taste death in the air.

When she inhaled, Veronica felt the rhodenine particles in the atmosphere drawing into her body, into her spirit. She felt their power, their ancient trails leading back to a time and place Veronica had never been to.

An explosion. The destruction of something. The destruction of a planet.

Veronica shuddered at the thought. She suddenly felt her thoughts, her emotions, start to untether from herself.

She exhaled slowly, cautiously, deliberately focusing on the blades in her hands as she siphoned the rhodenine from herself to the weapons.

When she felt the rhodenine leave her body, she opened her eyes and saw the purple lines in the blades were now glowing with the ancient power of the rhodenine.

She spun the blade in her right hand toward the bars of Luena's cage, and the blade cut through the iron bars without effort.

She cut a hole in the cage and waited for Luena to crawl out. At first, the woman hesitated, staring at Veronica as if she was a hunter who had caught their prey. But once Veronica stepped to the side and motioned for Luena to come out, to escape, the woman crawled through the cut bars and slowly stood to face her rescuer.

"Why would you bother coming back to save my life? You could have escaped this horrible place, but instead, you came back to rescue me."

Veronica shrugged. "My job is to save lives. It's what I've always done. You would have done the same for me."

Luena shook her head. "Not a chance. Knowing what that freak...that monster...Simper is capable of..." her gaze wandered to the floor. "I would have escaped this place the first chance I was given."

Veronica realized most people would have escaped without worrying too much about the others in captivity with them.

This is what made Veronica different. What made the Lazerblades different.

Veronica spun the blades on the axis of the handles. They felt natural to her. They felt awesome. The power flowing through them felt endless. Ancient. Chaotic. "Where did he take them? The others."

"Deeper underground, where the sacrificial altar is."

"This place runs deeper?"

Luena nodded. "Simper said the closer to the planet's core he could get, the closer he would be to the Ancient Ones."

"How do I get down there?"

Luena let out an exhausted huff. Tears filled her eyes. She buried her face in her palms.

Veronica wanted to hug her, to comfort her, but this was beyond a hug or a placating comment. This woman needed deep therapy.

She moved a shaky arm out and pointed toward the other side of the dungeon. "There's a ladder that leads down a hole. Deeper into darkness."

Veronica nodded. "Okay. I'll be back."

Luena shrugged. "I can't leave this place. This is my end."

"It's not," Veronica growled. "You need to leave. If you're

not gone by the time I come back, I'll see you out myself."

Luena looked at Veronica, sadness filling her eyes. Then she got down on the floor and crawled back into the cage.

"You said you would escape the first chance you got. You would leave others behind. And now you crawl back into the cage?!"

Luena buried her head in her knees and sat in that corner, saying nothing.

Veronica made her way to the other side of the dungeon, double-checking each cage to make sure nobody else needed rescuing.

When she reached the other end of the room, she found another trap door, much like the one in the garden. She lifted the hatch and looked down another hole with another ladder. She wasn't sure how deep Simper's empire went. She also knew that if she ventured down there, there was a chance she might not be able to return up here. Simper could have anything down there. What if he had all the prisoners ready to ambush her? What if Veronica was to be the sacrifice to the Ancient Ones?

She ventured down the ladder, attempting to hold onto the railing with a blade handle in each of her hands. She made a mental note that she would need to craft herself a holster of some kind to carry these things on her back.

The purple glow of the blade etchings lit up the tight passageway as Veronica ventured deeper underground.

When her feet touched the bottom, she found herself in another narrow corridor, which she took to another open chamber.

Beyond the entrance, she saw a stone setting in the center of the chamber, a square block that was stained in blood. A beam of sunlight poured down from the ceiling onto the block, illuminating the tan-colored stone and the particles of dust that had been disturbed in this place either by her or by whomever had entered this place before her. How sunlight could get down into a place like this was beyond her. Had Simper simply drilled a half dozen holes through the planet's surface to make his maze of hideouts down here?

She smelled the coppery scent of blood. This was a trap. There was something lingering there in the shadows, in the dark recesses of that open expanse, beyond the beam of sunlight, but she didn't know what. She could sense Simper in this place, but more than that, she could sense all the evil surrounding him.

She squared her shoulders and tightened her grip on the handles of her Scion blades.

One way or another, he would fall. If she fell with him, so be it.

She entered the chamber.

Nothing happened when she stepped her foot across the threshold. She stepped onto grimy stone and entered the massive chamber without incident. She cautiously made her way toward the stained block in the center. The sunlight was inviting, cutting through the darkness like a blade.

She gripped her blade handles tighter, expecting Simper or the enslaved girls to leap out of the shadows and destroy her.

As she neared the stone setting, she could see strange etchings on the floor…etchings similar to the ones carved into the black door she had walked through.

This place had something to do with the Ancient Ones.

Veronica stepped into the sunlight. Her blades suddenly flew out of her hands and clanged across the other side of the room. A force pushed Veronica to sit on the stone block.

A loud rumble shook the room, and Veronica watched as stone blocks lifted out of the floor throughout the room. Girls were chained to each one, shackles on their wrists and ankles.

The same prisoners from the dungeon.

The stone Veronica sat on shook and started to rise. She

117

scrambled on top of it, struggling to find her balance as she grabbed for purchase on the block.

"Don't fall yet, Veronica." It was Simper's voice, echoing throughout the chamber. "You still have to fulfill my deepest desires, and you can't do that if you're dead."

"What?"

Simper slipped out of the shadows and looked up at her from the ground floor. He motioned to the chained girls all around him. "I am going to sacrifice them to the Ancient Ones. Then I am going to plead with them to spare your life and give you to me. We will live together, forever my love. We will create life for the Ancient Ones."

Veronica gnashed her teeth together and scanned the room for her blades. She couldn't see them in the dark shadows anywhere.

The stone stopped shifting upward. She was at least twenty feet high above the ground now. Vertigo threatened to dispel her, but she managed to kneel and get a decent grip on the edges of the stone pillar to keep her balance.

She looked down at Simper.

His beady eyes looked up at her, his irises glimmering with the beams of sunlight. "Get ready, my love. For now is the time this world becomes ours."

CHAPTER 10

A Final Confrontation

Veronica saw Simper close his eyes. Rumbling echoed from above her and she realized the openings in the ceiling that had been allowing sunlight into the chamber were closing up, allowing the darkness to engulf them. Simper produced an orb full of a bright white light edged in black and sent it into the air as the room became aglow in a dark haze.

"It is time for your lives to mean something. It is time for you to give those lives over to the Ancient Ones!"

Veronica felt a buzz in the air. Energy crackled, and she felt the whole room begin to shake. Dust and debris sprinkled on her from the ceiling.

She wished David were here. She wished Carrie was here. She wished her brother was here. Anyone to help her. But she was on her own and the feeling left her empty. How could she kill him?

The openings in the ceiling that once allowed sunlight to breach this realm now opened and allowed red beams to tear down through the mist, illuminating the girls who were scattered on the pillars around Veronica. Their bodies convulsed with agony as the red light touched their malnourished forms.

What was in that red beam? Was it a laser?

Simper raised his hands up to the ceiling and smiled wide. "Thank you, oh Ancient Ones for granting me the power to do your will. Accept these offerings as your slaves, as a sacrifice to you!"

The women writhed and cried out.

Veronica tried to block out the cacophony echoing throughout the chamber, tried to ignore the screams so she could decide how to deal with Simper, but the sounds were too great, too dire.

These poor girls had been taken, beaten, used. All under Veronica's nose. Under the nose of the Lazerblades.

Veronica stood tall on the pillar and peered down at Simper. He was awash in darkened light, but his eyes glowed red.

He had been responsible for all of this.

He had to be stopped.

She pointed down at him. "You'll die today!"

She slid onto her stomach and hugged the pillar. Then she slid down it like it was a fire pole, the rough texture of the stone scratching her stomach, thighs, and arms, spreading pain through her abdomen.

She reached the bottom and turned to face Simper. He was elsewhere in the room now, on the other side. She ran in that direction, but when she got there, he was suddenly on the other side of the room, opposite her.

He cackled, his laugh pinpricking Veronica's spine with its tone and audacity.

Instead of pursuing his teleporting form, she ran to the other corner of the room. She found the Scion blades laying on the ground, the metal of the blades reflecting the light emanating from the orb.

She lifted the weapons in her hands, gripping the handles

of the weapons as if they were an extension of herself.

She turned and found herself face-to-face with Simper, his black beady eyes a glowing red.

"You and I were always meant to be together. Don't you realize that?" He pulled something from his robe and shoved it into her face, smashing flower petals into her nose and then rubbing the plant across her skin, along her neck and her arms.

She stumbled backwards, surprised at the attack. A faint buzzing filled her veins, and she suddenly felt lightheaded. Dizzy. Vulnerable.

She strengthened her grip on the blades as she took a few steps back and shook her head, attempting to cast the effects of the Eros plant off as if it were a scattering of raindrops.

Her knees buckled and she dropped to the floor.

"I am going to create something new for the Ancient Ones. We are going to create life this night."

Veronica's mind struggled to cram the panic back down into her gut, but it kept resurfacing. The effects of the flower were too great, too powerful. She felt her grip on the blades weaken. She felt her eyes fluttering, as if her body wanted to sleep, to slumber, to fold into sexual delight.

If she slept, if she slipped out of consciousness, she knew she would awaken to a nightmare of Simper's creation.

I can't fight this, she told herself. The buzzing coasted through her thighs, through her stomach, her arms.

But I can. The voice! Still and soft. Otherworldly, but somehow close to her.

As she closed her eyes, Veronica felt a light breeze brush across her skin. As it left, it carried away the buzzing, the tingling, the tendrils of erotic passion, leaving her whole.

At peace.

Healed.

In unison, all the girls in the room screamed out in terror as the red beams brightened. Veronica looked up in time to watch every girl collapse.

The red beams died out.

The orb burned out.

The room sat in complete darkness.

"A sacrifice," Simper grumbled. "The Ancient Ones will feast on those souls tonight. And I will feast on yours."

"No." Veronica stood to her feet. She took a deep breath and pulled the rhodenine from the air around her, then channeled it into the blades, the handles of which sat firmly in her grips. The blades glowed purple with rhodenine. "Tonight, you die, as does the evil you've brought to Anaisha."

She brought the blades down toward where she assumed he stood, but they only struck empty air.

A beam of black glowing energy shot across the space in front of her and hit her in the chest, slamming her against the wall.

"Ergh!" she grunted. She took a deep breath, an aching spreading across her ribcage. She waited for a moment, allowing her eyes to adjust to the darkness around her. The openings at the top of the chamber no longer poured red light into the room, but they did allow for a very faint echoing of the outside moonlight, washing away just enough of the darkness to where Veronica could now see the pillars, and the dead women atop them.

Simper.

She leaped toward him, blades spinning in her hands. He vaulted into the air to an impossible height and coasted over her, landing directly behind her. She knelt and spun as one of her blades carved a line through his clothing and skin, drawing blood.

He looked down at the surface wound and smiled.

Veronica charged at him, swinging her blades around as they cut through the air in front of her, flashing purple light around them. Simper leaped up and over her again, this time shoving his hands into her back as she flew into a pillar face first.

The blades flung out of her hands, and she fell to the ground, her nose bleeding.

"Get up!" Simper grabbed her by the back of her blouse and tugged her back to her feet, slamming her against the pillar again. Simper poured hot breath across her ear. "I took you in. I taught you. I cared for you. I did everything in my power to help you reach your potential. And the way you repay me is to try to kill the very hand that's been feeding you?

"I will kill you. I will kill your friends."

Veronica shoved him away from her and then scrambled for one of the blades lying on the ground. She grabbed the handle, lifted the blade in the air, and spun it in front of her, putting a barrier between both her and Simper.

"You stupid woman!" He lunged toward her again. This time, she raised her knee up into his crotch and he fell to the ground, clutching his groin.

"That's for what you just did to me. And this—" she reached down and grabbed him by the hair, slamming his face into her knee and sending him backwards to the ground, "is for what you did to those women." She spun the blade in her right hand, then brought it down on the back of his neck as the metal sliced through his spinal cord and lopped his head off. It hit the ground with a thud and rolled off to the side, into darkness.

His body collapsed to the ground.

Veronica fell to her knees, her heart racing madly. She dropped the blade to the ground with a loud clang.

The silence in the room became thick, almost suffocating.

Veronica buried her face in her knees and rocked herself, the reality of what she had just done striking her like lightning.

She murdered a man.

That was it.

He was dead.

It made her feel sick.

But he wasn't a man, she reminded herself. *He was a monster. And if I hadn't killed him, others would have died at his hands.*

Tears streamed down her face, but she wiped them away with a degree of confidence that what she had just done was for the greater good. It was to protect the innocent.

The surety that David would be disappointed snared her for but a moment, but she reminded herself that he was always on the peaceful side of things, and sometimes peace just wasn't going to be an option. There would have been no coexisting with Simper. There would have been no imprisoning him, not with the power he displayed. He didn't want to be rehabilitated. He didn't want to pledge allegiance to good.

Destruction was the only option to rid the world of Simper's brand of malevolence.

Minutes passed, and Veronica settled within herself that what she had done here today was the right thing. Whether anyone else would see it that way wasn't relevant. She knew she would be able to sleep at night knowing she had put a stop to Simper's ring of terror.

She was startled by a voice, a shout. "Veronica Amorou!" The tone of the voice was hoarse and sickening, as if it was echoing from the deepest parts of the planet in some pocket of dark void.

The chamber rumbled, particles of stone raining down from the ceiling. The pillars the women had been slain upon retracted

124

back into the ground, as did the tall pillar Veronica had ridden to the top of the room.

All that lay before her was a large chamber filled with corpses.

"You have destroyed your teacher, Simper Creed."

Veronica focused her vision around the room in an attempt to find the source of the voice, but it seemed to come from everywhere and nowhere all at once.

"Stop searching for us. We are the Ancient Ones. We do not exist on your plane of existence, and you are not worthy—yet—to see us face-to-face."

"What do you want," she asked, spinning the blades in her hands.

"You want to kill us, don't you? You are disgusted with what happened here."

She sneered. "Show me your face and I'll make short work of you."

"We have no face."

Silence filled the room.

She felt something shift through the space in front of her. Something occupied the air there, something temporal, spiritual, but she could see nothing, only feel the atmosphere around her move like a spring breeze.

"We are the creators of this world. We are the ones who built its foundation. We are the ones who move its machinery toward an inevitable end."

This voice, this being, wasn't the one who spoke to her in that calm, still voice multiple times. The one who helped her resist the Eros plant. The one who helped her resist the lustful effects of the demonic plant Simper used to destroy the souls of the poor women scattered around her.

No, this was someone—something—different. This creature

or being (she wasn't sure) was not the one who had assisted her.

"You seem confused."

Veronica let out an exasperated breath. "What do you want?"

"Sacrifice to us, as your predecessor did, and we will grant you the power you seek."

"I don't seek power."

"You do. Power to protect your friends. Power to stop the coming evil upon your plane of existence."

Veronica started across the room, toward the hallway that led back to the ladder that would take her to the floors above. She retrieved her other blade, which had somehow wound up on the other side of the room. She tried not to look at the dead women, their bodies now lifeless husks that once contained purity and innocence.

One particular girl caught Veronica's attention. She was older than the rest. Brown, scraggly hair. Her lifeless eyes stared out at Veronica, one of them pale, almost glowing in the dark with the reflection of the faint moonlight.

Luena.

Veronica felt rage build within her. "I told you to get out."

Claustrophobia settled into her chest, and knowing that Simper was dead, that there was nothing she could do to save anyone down here, she knew her time here was done.

She felt a ripple in the air around her, as if this being had shuddered at her dismissal of its offer.

"You will not walk away from us, Veronica. We are gods to be revered. Respected. Worshipped."

"No," she whispered. "You are not gods."

The air quaked around her. She felt it with the rattling of her bones, with the shifting of her muscles and flesh. It was then she realized this thing, this entity, could not reach her here.

"We will be watching you, Veronica. You and your friends."

***

When Veronica climbed up out of the last hole and reentered the garden of Simper's property, she tasted morning light. The air was crisp and chilly, and the scent of grass and roses carried on the breeze.

At first, she wasn't sure what to do about Simper's property but to leave it be. It seemed to pose no immediate threat now that he was dead. His corpse was so far underground that nobody would notice him missing.

But the women.

Veronica couldn't let the parents or friends or family of these girls to not have the closure they most assuredly needed and wanted.

In the end, Veronica alerted the authorities to Simper's place. Anonymously, of course. The police didn't bother looking for a murderer or trying to pin Veronica to anything. They tore through his property, finding all manner of evil, including torture devices, ancient texts speaking of human sacrifice, and the underground chambers that housed the corners of darkness his evil hid in. Everyone involved seemed satisfied that he was dead, and nobody really asked who had killed him. There was enough evidence tying him to the capture of the now deceased women, it was a case closed.

Veronica said nothing to her friends. How could she speak to them about this? How could she tell David that she had killed a man, even one who had hurt so many? There was blood on her hands, and it would now taint her for the rest of her life. But it was a taint she could live with. No more women would suffer at Simper's hands.

In the end, the families of the victims were alerted. Especially Luena's husband and children.

She hid the blades, far out of her own reach. She might need to call on them one day, but it wouldn't be today. It wouldn't be tomorrow, either.

She had to keep Simper, her time here, and her newfound skills a secret.

Even though closure had come to the situation of Simper Creed, something didn't sit right with Veronica. Something nagged at the corner of her mind, at the edges of her spirit.

The creature—the Ancient One—had mentioned a coming evil. Was it referring to Mr. Big coming back? Or was it referring to something so evil that Veronica couldn't possibly conceive of it quite yet?

Only time would tell.

www.ingramcontent.com/pod-product-compliance
Lightning Source LLC
Chambersburg PA
CBHW061251170626
46809CB00007B/2940